Sold To The Syndicate

THE BOTTICELLI BROTHERHOOD SERIES

J.L. QUICK

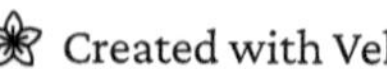 Created with Vellum

This novel is a contemporary mafia dark romance. It contains scenes and descriptive adult content that might be triggering for some readers.

Please ensure you read the trigger warnings prior to beginning this novel.

Trigger Warnings

Torture
Criminal Activity
Dubious/Non-Consensual Sexual Acts
Abduction/Captivity
Death
Edging/Orgasm Control
Gun Violence
Spanking
Profanity
Breeding
Impact Play
Bondage
Masturbation
Graphic Sexual Scenes
Exhibitionism
Knife/Blood Play
Breath Play

Chapter One

LORENZO

Crashing my hand into his face, the skin of my knuckles cracks as the skin above his eye splits. As my fist crashes into him once again, he lets out a pathetic moan. His blood beginning to spill down his face and my hand.

"This can end whenever you are ready to talk."

At this point, I know I am just toying with him, but I enjoy it. Ellis is so weak after the past few hours, that he is barely able to look up at me. I mostly just see his bloody, fluttering eyelids before his chin drops back down to his chest.

"For a piece of shit that couldn't keep his mouth shut about the family business, you sure seem to be holding your tongue now."

Someone has been destroying our safe houses and businesses – both legal and illegal. Once we realized that the serial arsonist was primarily targeting Botticelli business, we quickly determined that it was personal. Someone was coming for the family. After a few places known only to the family were set on fire, we realized that the information regarding just what businesses we own must be coming from someone on the inside. It took a few months, but thanks in part to some well-planted lies, we think we have finally found our mole.

"If you want this to end, you are going to need to tell me who the fuck you've been talking to."

"I can't," Ellis replies, his voice trembling as though he is about to cry, "They will kill me."

"You stupid fuck," I glare back at him, while picking my knife back up from the table, "I'm going to fucking kill you if you don't start talking."

Shifting the knife in my hand, becoming comfortable with its feel in my grip, I slowly bring it down his chest. His screams are of pure agony as my knife shifts from the tip to the blade, slowly fileting a sliver of skin from his chest. It is a stark contrast to the smile of pure euphoria slowly spreading across my face.

"I can't," Tears now roll down his face, as he continues to cry out, "They will kill my family."

Fuck... I might be a brutal son of bitch, but I am not going to kill his innocent wife and daughter. They won't be welcome in this city anymore, but I tend not to kill the innocent regardless of who they are connected to.

The knife in my hand beautifully separates another piece of his flesh from his body. Throwing his skin to the floor, I press my knife firmly against his neck.

"What makes you think I won't kill your fucking family?" My eyes narrow as I pose my question to him, "Maybe I'll even enjoy some time with that beautiful young wife of yours before I kill her."

His reaction takes me by complete surprise, and people rarely surprise me.

Ellis violently jerks in his chair, causing the knife in my hand to slice through the thin skin by his jugular. The self-inflicted wound is going to be just deep enough to be fatal. Slow as fuck, but fatal.

"Fuck," I grumble, throwing the knife to the ground, as I watch his blood pump from his neck.

Back to square fucking one...

"Get rid of this piece of shit," I bark at the other men in the room, "And then tell his family to get the fuck out of town. I need to go talk to Sal."

Storming out of the warehouse, I quickly cross the parking lot to my Maserati, while wiping my bloody hands across my shirt. Turning over the engine, it growls when I put it in drive and stomp on the accelerator. Swerving in and out city traffic, my fist pounds against top of the steering wheel.

I am not upset that traitor is dead, but I am fucking pissed that he managed to get the better of me.

That shit does not happen to me.

I am Lorenzo Fucking Botticelli. My family is like fucking royalty. My father rules this city, and someday soon I will be its new king.

No one gets the better of me. Fucking, no one.

The gates open, as I pull towards the family estate. Abruptly, I park my car by the garage before storming into the house.

"Lorenzo! Finally! Come join us," a very inebriated voice calls from the living room.

"Not now, V," I huff back at her as I continue marching towards my father's office. Gaining my composure, I straighten my tie against my bloody shirt before knocking on the door.

I might be pissed off, but there is no way that I will barge into his office not showing this man the respect he is expecting – and deserves.

Chapter Two

AVALIE

Apparently, big dick energy doesn't always translate to the bedroom. I was closer to coming last night with my vibrator that wouldn't hold a charge.

Quietly sliding out of the bed, I look around in the dark for my clothes. I manage to find my purse, dress, and heels. After pulling my dress over my head, I fish through my purse to find my phone. I need the flashlight to find my panties. As I dig around, Matt – or was it Mark? – startles me when I hear him stirring in the bed. If I plan to leave without having to speak to him again, it is apparently going to be commando.

Fuck, I really liked that thong.

Stepping into the hallway, I try my hardest not to make a sound as I pull the door shut behind me. Relief floods over me when it barely even clicks as it closes. Digging my phone back out of my purse, I request an Uber before putting my heels back on and heading downstairs.

It might be two in the morning, but my ride will be here in about five minutes. That means I should make it home before three. Well before Frank wakes up for the day.

By the time I make it down all the stairs, the Uber is pulling up out front. With how little traffic there is at this hour, we make it to my destination within thirty minutes. Leaving my driver a five star review, because he was hilarious and a gentleman, I climb out of the backseat.

My stomach drops when I notice that the lights are still on in our apartment. He is either passed out in the living room or he has not been to sleep yet. Either way, I am completely fucked when I walk in that door.

Taking my time, I slowly take the stairs to the sixth-floor walk-up. I hesitate to put my keys in the door, wanting one more moment to myself. The little moment I wanted is taken from me as I watch the handle turn and the door open.

"Where the fuck have you been?" His hand grabs my wrist tightly, yanking me into the apartment before he slams the door shut.

Based on the current aroma of this room and his demeanor, I quickly come to realization that he has not been to sleep yet. Every breath he exhales in my direction reeks of cheap booze.

His eyes gaze over my body in sheer disgust.

Parting my lips to answer him, my words are silenced by the back of his hand slamming against my cheek. No tears well in my eyes. Not a sound passes from my lips. I refuse to give him the satisfaction of knowing he hurt me ever again.

"Is that all you've got?" I spit back at him before he backhands me again.

"Whoring your way around the city," he releases his grip on my wrist, disgustedly pushing me away from him, "just like your fucking mother."

He isn't entirely wrong. When I was seven, she left his abusive ass for some guy she had just met. Frank rambles about it every time he gets drunk, which is often. We have not seen her since. While I will never forgive her for leaving me here with him, I do not fault her for needing to get out of this house. I think, in a way, I have been trying to get the hell out here the same way. Getting me away from this hell that is my life with Frank.

Yet, in the most fucked up of ways, I am grateful for him. He is not my dad. I was just extra baggage that came along with my mom, but when she left, he let me stay. I work in his produce store and I put up with his bullshit. In exchange, I have a roof over my head and food on my table, most of the time. Until I manage to save enough money to provide those things for myself, this is just my life.

I don't feel sorry for me. And I definitely do not want anyone else to feel sorry for me. A life with Frank has not made me a timid little mouse of a woman. I am fearless when it comes to my words and actions, because I know that no one in this world can hurt me any worse than Frank has over the years.

"Are you even fucking listening to me?" his words slice through my thoughts. "I expect you downstairs at eight to open the store."

Stomping towards his room, I can hear him mumbling to himself, "No one is ever going to take you off my hands if you keep fucking every guy you meet."

Six guys. According to Frank, having really shitty sex with six different guys makes me a whore.

Grabbing a bag of peas for my cheek, I head to my room to try to get a few hours of sleep before I need to open the store for Frank. Exchanging my dress for an oversized t-shirt, I set my alarm before climbing into bed.

Chapter Three

LORENZO

"Come in," his deep voice billows from the other side of the door.

Pushing open the door, I step into the office to see my father diligently working at his desk.

Noting the tiredness on his face, "You're up late, Papa."

"There is always work to be done, Lorenzo," his eyes gaze towards the door, silently instructing me to close it behind me, "and I don't trust that guy out there with your sister any further than I could throw him."

I snicker. Venecia is his baby, and on top of that she is the only girl in the family. I do not think he will ever trust any man to be alone with her.

"Come," he gestures, "Sit. Tell me what you got out of Ellis."

Knowing he is going to be disappointed, I break eye contact with him before responding, "Nothing."

The look on his face confirms his disappointment, and he does not like to be let down.

"It was definitely him. He was the mole," I continue before he has the opportunity to speak, "but he would not talk. Whoever he was talking to had him scared absolutely shitless."

"More afraid than he was of us? Of you?"

"Yes," nodding along with my response, "he was more afraid of what they would do to his family than anything I had done, or was willing to do, to him."

"Someday son, when you are in charge, you are going to have to make a call that ends the life of a woman or a child."

"You might be right, but today is not that day."

"If you want to retain power in this world, people cannot know you have a weakness. They will exploit it every chance they get."

"I know, Papa."

And I do. I know he is right.

"I sent Marco to go take care of them," he nonchalantly replies to me.

He stands, walking around the desk to place a hand on my shoulder. It is not a consoling touch. Instead, it is a firm squeeze, reminding me who is in charge of this family.

"Next time, I expect you to handle things accordingly. People will not disrespect this family, and you will not give them a reason to think we are soft or that they can disrespect us," releasing his grip he walks towards the door, "I am heading to bed. Keep an eye on your sister."

"Yes, Papa."

His disappointment looms over me even after he has left the room.

We will never agree that my unwillingness to kill the innocent is a weakness, and that is something I will never understand about him. I lost my mother, his wife, solely because someone took her to hurt the family. And it did just that. My father nearly took down the entire city trying to get his revenge. It also nearly ended our family. V, Carlo and I were all sent to live with family in Italy for several years after her death, while he waged a war of pure vengeance.

I will play by his rules while he is still the one in charge, but I refuse to lose this last little piece of who I am. He spent his life grooming me to be the man I am.

The man he needed me to be to take over for him – a brutal man that has no remorse for torturing and killing our enemies.

Fuck remorse, I enjoy it. Seeing how far you can push the human body is fucking exhilarating. When done right, it's the biggest fucking turn on there is.

Leaving my father's office, I pull the door shut before heading into the living room. After all, I promised Papa that I would keep an eye on his princess. I probably should shower and change first, but I feel that the blood splattering my clothes and staining my hands will have more impact on this guy that my father is concerned about.

Entering the living room, I see V sitting on the lap of the guy my father mentioned. To describe him simply, he looks like he would be the captain of the lacrosse team. One hand around her waist, and the other is a lot higher on the inside of her thigh than it should be. His face is against her neck as he boldly whispers things he probably shouldn't be thinking into her ear.

Crossing the room, I walk to the bar to pour myself a bourbon. With my drink in hand, I turn towards V and lean against the bar. Slowly sipping the warm liquor, I glare at Lacrosse, his hand slowly inching closer to a place that will cause him to lose it. It is not until I clear my throat that I garner his attention.

His eyes go wide when he sees me, quickly taking in my appearance. The hand, once high on my sister's thigh, now quickly resting well below her knee.

"Rough day at work?" V jokes as she slides from his lap to give me a hug, "You could have at least cleaned up first."

"I wanted to come and meet your friend," I say, nodding my head towards Lacrosse.

She gestures to him to join us over at the bar, "This is Chad."

Of course it fucking is.

Nervously, he walks towards us. I am certain that my current appearance, coupled with the fact that I tower over his large athletic frame, makes me seem intimidating to him.

Good. I want him to be afraid of what will happen if he touches her, without having to say a word.

Before I can say anything, the petite brunette previously sitting on the couch is pressing herself past V to get close to me.

"And I'm Jessica," she says placing one hand on my chest and the other out to shake my hand.

Being polite, I gently accept her hand and introduce myself, "I'm Lorenzo, V's brother."

Her hand lingers on my chest as she reaches for my glass of bourbon.

"No," I pull the glass from her reach, "I don't share. And you don't want to play with me, little girl."

Sensually inching her fingers up my chest, to the collar of my jacket, she stares into my eyes. With the fire burning behind her eyes, it is more than apparent what she wants.

"I am not a little girl," she whispers, as she pulls on the lapel of my jacket.

I dip my thumb into my glass of bourbon before gently dragging it along her lower lip. She takes a deep breath and parts her lips, allowing me to slide my thumb into her mouth. She takes it willingly and sensually sucks the bourbon from my thumb, never breaking her lusty gaze at me.

Looking down at her, my thumb still in her mouth, I grip her chin. Her eyes narrow and I can smell her excitement. My grip tightens, forcing her mouth open. She opens wider trying to decrease the pressure of my grip. In return, I squeeze harder and demandingly pull her face towards mine. The fire in her eyes slowly being replaced with fear.

"You might not be a little girl," my voice a deep whisper, as I continue my strong hold, never breaking eye contact with her. She does not know what she is asking for, and she needs to know that my pleasure also comes with pain, "but you are not ready to play with the big boys."

Tears begin pooling in her eyes, as a little spittle begins to roll down her chin.

She definitely cannot handle what I need from her. What I would demand from her.

Releasing her, she stumbles back from me as I turn towards V.

"It's late," my voice flat as I take the last sip of my drink, "get one of the guys to take your friends home."

Placing my glass on the bar, I head towards the stairs to go to bed. I do not worry about V following my directions, and at this point I know her friends are both ready to leave.

Chapter Four

AVALIE

The blaring alarm clock coming from my phone rouses me from my sleep.

"Ugh! It's too fucking early," I groan to myself, rubbing the sleep from my eyes while slowly climbing out of the bed.

Throwing off the shirt I slept in, I grab a bra from the floor before throwing on a tight v-neck, short jean shorts and a pair of sneakers.

My hair is still holding the curls from last night, so I pull it into a loose high ponytail. Grabbing a few different brushes, I put on a little makeup.

It really is true. Last night's winged-liner can be today's smoky eye.

Taking one last look in the mirror, I grab my zip-up hoodie and keys. Walking down the stairs, I glance at my phone and see I only have about ten minutes to get the store open. Frank will have my ass if he finds out I was late. I pick up my speed, traversing the stairs two at a time, and walk briskly around the block.

Rounding the corner, I see the store – Taylor's Produce. I have grown up here and the people of this neighborhood are like family. Everyone is always stopping in to chat and grab a thing or two. Truth be told, if it weren't for Frank, I would actually enjoy working here.

Bending down, I unlock the roll-up gate. Using my momentum of standing back up, I lift the gate hoping it catches and stays open. Catching it as it begins to roll back down, I squat a little and thrust my arms over my head for my second attempt. It still does not latch.

What I would give to be tall, or just taller, one day in my life. To just once be able to reach the top shelf on my own!

Reaching up, I brace to absorb the impact of the falling gate again. This time it stops before it gets to me.

It is only when I catch the scent of cologne that I realize someone is standing immediately behind me. Spinning around, I startle when my face hits his chest. With one large hand, he is effortlessly pushing the gate into the box over the door.

"I had it," I huff at him, bending back down to pick my things up from the sidewalk.

"That was obvious," the voice is deep and smooth.

Grabbing my keys and phone, I notice the smooth voice is wearing some very nice shoes – too nice for this neighborhood. My eyes scroll up his body as I slowly stand back up.

The grey herringbone trousers he is wearing are immaculately pressed and made for his massive body. My gaze continues to move up him, and even through the pants it is impossible not to recognize the massive muscular tree trunks this man has for thighs. When my eyes travel further up him, I swallow.

No, I gulped and got tingly.

It's obviously just something in his pocket. Like what, Ava? A water bottle? A flashlight? A fucking traffic cone?

Realizing I am squatting at eye-level with this man's crotch as I mentally try to determine what the bulge in his pants is, I quickly stand up straight. Even fully standing, I have only made it to eye level with his chest, which is comparatively as massive as his thighs. His chest is only further accentuated by his broad shoulders and the pristinely pressed white button-down shirt hugging his torso.

My eyes continue from his muscular frame to his face. He has a broad jaw and chiseled cheekbones that put

Cillian Murphy to shame. When I meet his eyes, they nearly take my breath away. They are hazel, but like a golden caramel. I have never seen anything like them in my life.

As though he is oblivious to the fact that I just eye-fucked him, he flatly states, "I'm looking for Frank."

"I'm sorry," I bumble back, "we aren't open yet and Frank isn't here."

"I didn't ask if you are open. I clearly said I needed to speak with Frank."

Putting my keys in the door, I unlock it and push it open to step inside.

"And I clearly said Frank isn't here," I sternly repeat, pushing the door shut behind me.

Only it doesn't shut. His large hand is pressed against the door and he is holding it open. Trying to press it shut is useless. His sheer size alone, I am no match for his strength.

"Let Frank know that I will be back this afternoon," his voice is stern and demanding, "and he better be here."

"And who are you?"

"Just tell him Sal sent me. Do you think you can remember that *piccola pesca*?" he lets go of the door and has disappeared down the sidewalk as quickly as he arrived.

"Picco...what," I mumble to myself.

Did he just fucking swear at me?

Pushing the door shut, I lock it before dropping my things on the counter. It only takes me a few minutes to get the store ready to open. Promptly at eight, I unlock the door and put up the open sign.

Chapter Five

LORENZO

My morning is spent driving around the city collecting various debts for the family – mostly gambling and loans. It has been a relatively uneventful morning, with everyone promptly paying up on the debts they owe or providing us with information regarding the other families.

Everyone except Frank. He has always been a problem, and he is the reason I am out here doing a job that we should be able to send almost any one of the guys out to take care of. Yet, he has somehow been managing to avoid them for the past month – just like he managed to avoid me this morning.

After a few more stops, including one at Carmine's for lunch, I intend to head back over there. Hopefully that petite little blonde with the perky ass passed on my message to Frank because I do not intend to have to come back to this shitty area of the city again.

Although, seeing that round ass peeking out of those little shorts does make the trip back almost worthwhile.

It is a little after two in the afternoon when I make my way back across town to the little produce store to get Frank to pay up. Parking at the first open spot I see on the block, I climb out and begin walking towards the store.

Frank spots me as I approach and hurries inside. Sprinting the last few feet, I shove my body into the door frame before he has a chance to close it. Pushing myself inside, I close and lock the door behind me.

"We don't need to make this difficult, Frank," my words dry as I slowly stalk towards him.

With every step I take, he continues to back away from me until he has backed himself against the register.

"I...I don't have it," Frank stammers at me.

"Frank," I walk close enough to him to grab a fistful of his shirt, "you owe the Botticellis a lot of fucking money. We don't just forget about half a million dollars."

"M...m...maybe we can work something out."

"We aren't a fucking bank, Frank," I pull on his shirt, lifting his feet off the ground and throwing him onto the counter, "We don't do payment plans."

As his body slides across the counter, he collides with all of the items on it, taking everything with him as he falls to the ground on the other side. The sound of him and everything else hitting the ground echoes throughout the small store.

"Frank," a feminine voice calls from the back of the store, "everything okay up there?"

I can hear the delicate pad of her feet walking towards the front of the store as Frank stands up, obviously disheveled, from behind the counter.

Her eyes widen as she walks around aisle and takes us both in. As if unfazed, she continues to walk towards Frank.

"Everything is fine," he blurts out through his cracked lip, "Go clean up in the back."

"Are you sure...?," Her words interrupted by his hand crashing across her face.

"I said to go clean up in the back," he yells at her.

I am in such shock at her lack of reaction to his strike that I almost fail to grab his wrist before he attempts to bring his hand across her face again.

"Go," I demand, as I gesture for her to leave us.

"Fine," she grabs a bag and stomps towards the front door, "fucking fend for yourself, Frank."

That ass. That mouth. How his strike barely phased her. I'd be lying to myself if I didn't admit that from our two short interactions, she intrigues the fuck out of me. She is unlike all of the soft and subservient women I normally meet.

She opens the door and within seconds she is gone.

No longer interrupted, my thoughts are immediately back on Frank.

Using my hold on his wrist, I yank his body back onto the counter. Flipping him onto his back, I press my forearm against his throat while leaning down into his face.

"As I was saying," my voice low and firm, "we don't just forget a debt like yours."

He struggles as I press my body onto him, using my weight to further limit his ability to breathe.

"I will give you this evening, but I need you to understand that we will be back tomorrow to collect. If you don't have it all, you better have something and a fucking good plan to take care of the rest of it really fucking fast."

Sliding my forearm from his throat to his chest, "Do you understand Frank?"

He nods back at me.

Gripping his shirt as I lift his body from the counter, "I'm sorry, Frank, but I am going to need a fucking answer out of you."

"I understand."

"See you tomorrow," I smile as I release my grip on his shirt, causing his body to fall back to the counter.

Opening the door, I step out onto the sidewalk. Before beginning the walk to my car, I look in the opposite direction to see if the petite blonde is still around. No sign of her.

Once back in my car, my phone buzzes in my pocket. Pulling it out of my pocket, I see a text from Marco.

MARCO

Vixen's has been hit.

"Fuck," I grumble before texting him back.

Be there in thirty. We need to end these assholes.

Chapter Six

AVALIE

Fuck Frank. Fuck this shit.

In the past couple of hours, I have walked nearly every street in the neighborhood trying to clear my head and calm down. It is not working, because the resounding thought in my head is 'fuck this.'

Figuring Frank will be at the store for at least a few more hours, I head back to the apartment so I can lock myself in my room before he gets back.

Entering the apartment, I am relieved that I was right and he is not yet home. Grabbing a couple of bottles of water and some snacks, I head to my bedroom. After locking the door, I pull the dresser in front of it just in case he comes home more pissed off than he was at the store today.

Flopping onto the bed, the mattress creeks underneath me.

"What the fuck am I going to do?"

Pulling my purse from the floor, I dig around in it for my phone. Entering my information, I log into my bank account.

$4,283.88.

That is not going to get me far in this city.

Fuck it! I can't do this shit anymore.

Frank will pay me tomorrow for this past week. It won't be much, but I don't want to leave without it. Every little bit is going to help.

I'll just figure it out from there.

Pulling a duffle bag from my closet, I cannot believe that I am actually doing this. After all this time, I am finally going to do it. I am going to leave.

Slowly, I sort through my things. This bag is only going to hold so much. Lucky for me, I don't own that much and when I am done not that much is actually getting left behind.

Zipping up the duffel bag, I place it on the floor of my closet and shut the door before glancing around the room. There are enough things left behind that with a quick glance you would never realize I packed away most of my belongs.

Good. In the event he does come in here tomorrow, I don't want Frank to have any idea what I am planning.

Removing my shorts and bra, I climb under the blankets before pulling up an eBook on my phone. Scrolling through my library, I settle on a romance novel. Snuggling into the blankets and getting comfortable, my fingers start scrolling through the pages.

While flipping through the dedication and prologue, I briefly wonder if this is why I feel like sex is so unrewarding. In every book I read, these women have repeated mind-blowing, earth-shattering orgasms with the men they fuck. I am starting to think that does not actually happen. Complete bullshit. If you want it done right, you just need to do it yourself.

Fuck it. At least I'll have some good motivation.

Somewhere around chapter four my plans of reading all night get derailed.

Damn this is spicy for a rom-com!

All of this reading about passionate kisses, sensual caresses, and firm strokes of the tongue has left me unable to ignore the needy tingle between my thighs.

After removing my panties, I pull my rabbit from the nightstand. Flipping it on, I slide it beneath the covers before picking up my phone with my free hand. Gently rubbing the vibrating head in circles over my clit, I continue to read.

Tossing my phone to the bed, I use my now free hand to throw back the blankets on top of me. The vibrator circling my clit is no longer enough. My thighs spread, allowing me the access to provide what my body so desperately needs.

My pussy so wet that I slide the vibe inside of me effortlessly, stopping only when the rabbit ears are resting on my clit. The pulsing inside of me and flutters on my clit have me barely able to breathe. Arching my back, my hips rock firmly against the toy in my hand while I lift my shirt releasing my breasts.

Pulling the vibrator from me, I bring it up to my chest and place it on my already tight nipple. Still coated in my moisture, it easily glides back and forth over my nipple. In response to the vibrations on my chest, my pussy clenches. The tingling sensation of my clit demanding a release causes me to let out a light moan.

Without hesitation, I thrust the pulsing vibrator inside of me and firmly press it the vibrating ears against my clit. Pinching and pulling on my nipple, I writhe around the toy vibrating between my thighs. Continuing to rock my hips against my hand, I can feel the release building in my core.

A slight arch of my back, and it hits all of the right places. Pulling hard on my nipple, my mouth falls open as I begin to see stars behind my eyes. An airy scream rises from my chest as I convulse around the toy deep inside of me.

Still shaking and breathing heavy, I slowly pull it from me and turn it off.

I need to remember to pack that!

My heart is racing as I catch my breath.

Fuck men. They definitely cannot do what that little rabbit can.

Just as my heart stops racing, there is a knock on my door and a jiggle of the handle that startle me.

"Ava"

"It's locked Frank," I yell back after collecting myself, "What do you want?"

"I...um...I just wanted to say I was sorry for earlier," his words obviously slurred even through the door.

"That's great," I sarcastically reply.

"See you at the store at eight."

What the fuck was that? In all the years I have known Frank, not once has he apologized for being an abusive asshole.

Chapter Seven

LORENZO

Traffic is horrible this morning, and it is taking longer than anticipated for Luca and me to get across town. At least if this ride is going to take forever, I am stuck with my childhood best friend. We have grown up in this family together, and when the day comes that I am in charge he knows he will be my right-hand man.

While stuck in the car, our conversations cross all topics – women, the Yankees, the new guy driving for V.

I wanted to get to Frank's early, before it was full of customers. We have enough cops in our pocket that they would look the other way if I beat the piss out of him with witnesses, but the family tries to maintain as much of an upstanding reputation as we can.

And that means no witnesses.

When we finally pull up in front of the store just after nine, I am pleasantly surprised to see Frank through the window. This might go easier than I had originally thought. Entering the store with Luca, he shields the bat behind his large frame when we realize there is one elderly customer inside.

Casually strolling from the door, I browse like any other slow shopper until the elderly woman leaves. As soon as she steps out of the store, Luca flips the deadbolt on the door.

"Good morning, Frank," I smirk walking towards the register, "For your sake, I hope you stumbled into some money last night."

"I don't ha-," his words halted by Luca's bat crashing down on the counter, causing the register and baskets to shake.

"Yesterday, I thought you said you understood," my words gruff as Luca pushes the bat into his chest.

Frank whimpers back, "I don't have your money, but I have something else."

"You don't have shit, Frank," Luca shoves him with the barrel of the bat, "If you had anything worth a damn, we wouldn't be here right now. We would have taken it from you already."

"Bu…But I do," Frank stammers back, "It should cover all of what I owe. Maybe even more."

Walking around the counter, grabbing him with both hands by the shirt, I lift him off the ground and shove him against the wall.

"Don't fuck with us Frank," I snarl in his face, "You can either pay up or Luca is going to enjoy getting in quite a few swings before we leave to come back and do this again tomorrow."

Lowering Frank to the ground, I pull him around the counter so that he is in front of Luca, who looks like a kid at the batting cage eager to start swinging. Stepping out of the way, I make room for him to do so and he does not hesitate. Within seconds the bat slams into the left side of Frank's torso. The sound of his ribs cracking is audible, like the crackle of small sticks.

Blubbering for air and clutching his side, Frank falls to his knees. Before he has a chance to react, I am standing in front of him and using his hair to firmly tilt his face up towards mine. Seeing the fear in his eyes, it is clear that he can see the killer in mine.

"Ava…," he struggles to speak through the pain in his side, "I can give you Ava."

"Who the fuck is Ava?" Luca retorts, poking him with the bat.

"Avalie. The blonde," he grunts and rasps, "the blonde girl that was here yesterday."

"You mean your daughter?" I question, as Frank nods his head in agreement.

"Why would we want your daughter?" Luca quips back before I have a chance to stop him.

"She's not my daughter," Frank struggles to reply, "She's just some kid that got left with me. She's pretty..."

Luca looks to me when Frank stops speaking to catch his breath.

"You could sell her," Frank pushes out through painful breaths, "or you could keep her."

"We don't-," Luca stops when I shoot a glance at him.

His offering is not conventional, at least not for our family. We refuse to delve into the skin trade. Yet, I am considering it. She intrigues me – the way she took that hit yesterday and subsequently told him to fuck off – I have never met a woman like that before. The women I meet are either timid or pretending to have the gall that she does, but when it comes down to it, they all crumble and cannot take what I need to give them.

"Fine," I release his hair and shove him away from me, "We will take her. As of now she is Botticelli property and we will do with her as we see fit."

Frank does not even blink at my words. While I know she will be well cared for, he is completely unfazed by the unknown future that he just sold her into.

"So...," his voice trembling, "we are good?"

"Where is she?"

"She's out back going through this morning's delivery."

"Then we are good," I pause, "as soon as Luca breaks your leg. We do, after all, have a reputation to uphold."

A big grin spreads across Luca's face. He enjoys inflicting pain nearly as much as I do.

"When you're done," I nod to Luca, "meet me out back with the car."

He nods back at me, and the last thing I see before walking towards the storeroom is Luca prepping to swing his bat. A pathetic scream echoes through the store as I reach the exit to the alley.

Stepping into the alley, Avalie is bent over and rummaging through a crate. Distracted from the bottom of her ass peaking from her shorts, I momentarily lick my lips.

"What are you doing back here?" she questions when she sees me.

"I am here to collect a debt."

"That's Frank. He is inside," she scoffs, "I don't owe you shit."

"That is where you are wrong, *piccola pesca*," my words deliberately slow, "you are going to be the payment."

"Excuse me," she snaps back.

"Frank gave you to us to pay off what he owed," stepping closer, "You belong to the Botticelli family now."

"The fuck I do," she chucks the apple in her hand at my face, "I don't belong to anyone."

"Someone let the brat out of the bag today," I take another step towards her as Luca pulls the car down the alley blocking her only means of escape, "Let me be clearer, you *belong* to the Botticelli family now."

Throwing another apple at me, she turns to run. She only makes it few steps before my hand is firmly wrapping around the back of her neck and pulling her body back towards me. Once she is against me, I firmly wrap one arm around her waist and the other around her neck.

She struggles to free herself, but without much effort. I am no match for her small stature. It does not stop her though. She continues to thrash against me, kicking my shins when I lift her off the ground to her carry towards the car.

Chapter Eight

AVALIE

This cannot be happening. I was out of this shit in just a few hours. Starting over with a new life.

Traffic Cone's thick muscular arms are tightly wrapped around my neck and waist. I struggle to pull from his hold, but he is ridiculously stronger than me. As I struggle, he lifts me off the ground with ease. Trying to take advantage of what little leverage I have, I swing my feet trying desperately to kick him in the shins. Just maybe I will kick him hard enough that he will loosen his grip long enough for me to get away.

"She looks feisty," the other guy calls from the open window of the driver's seat.

"Would you just open the trunk?" Traffic Cone groans back to him.

"You are not putting me in the fucking trunk!" I yell back as I continue to struggle. Throwing my head back, I hear Traffic Cone grunt as I make contact with his face.

Relief washes over me when the guy driving opens the back door instead of the trunk.

"I don't put pretty girls in my trunk," the driver responds to me, "but if you don't calm the fuck down, I'm pretty sure Renzo is going to force me to make an exception for you."

"Try that shit again, and you will definitely be going in the trunk."

His arms still firmly wrapped around me, Renzo slides into the back seat pulling me in with him. Sliding me off his lap, he pushes me across the backseat to the other side of the car before pulling the car door shut.

He then slides across the seat until he is next to me with his thigh pressed up against mine. My body tenses and I stop fighting as he slowly leans close, so close his broad chest touches my arm and I can feel his warm breath blow across my cheek. My heart begins to race as his nose ever so slightly grazes my cheek as his arm reaches across me. Bringing his arm back across me, he pulls back with a smug expression on his face before buckling my seat belt.

"I don't think we'll need to put her in the trunk," his words as smug as his expression, as he yanks on the seatbelt tightening it around my waist, "I think she's going to listen like a good fucking girl."

My reaction to his words confuses me, but I know he is right. I huff and cross my arms, mumbling back, "Arrogant, fucking asshole."

Fighting back now is futile. I will wait. Save my energy now, so I can fight back when I need to. When I can get away.

"She is pretty cute when she pouts," the driver chuckles as he looks at me in the rearview mirror.

Ignoring his comment, Renzo flatly says, "Head over to Frank's apartment so we can pick up a few of her things."

The drive around the block is short, and we are quickly parking at the curb.

"Behave yourself," Renzo's eyes lock on mine, "Do not make me regret leaving you here with Luca."

He quickly steps from the car towards the apartment. Discretely, I slowly reach into the front pocket of my shorts for the small pocket knife I was using to open boxes. The door of the car has no more than shut when I hear the locks click.

Shit...

"Sorry pretty girl," he looks back at me in the mirror, "But I am not going to piss him off by letting you get the better of me."

Within minutes, Renzo is back at the car. Tossing in the bag I had packed last night, he climbs back into the backseat.

"Home," he nods at Luca before turning to face me. His fingers drum softly on my bag of things between us on the seat as his eyes linger between me and the bag.

"What?" I snidely question when I can no longer take his inquisitive gaze.

"You," his words slow and deep as he continues to drum his fingers over the bag, "You intrigue me *piccola pesca*. Where were you getting ready to run off to before Frank gave you to me?"

Pursing my lips, I refuse to answer his question. What I was planning to do is absolutely none of his business.

"What kind of girl has a bag of her things all nicely packed and ready to go? Did you know? Did Frank tell you his plan?"

I can feel his eyes continue to gaze over me as we drive through the city. Trying to ignore him, I focus my eyes on the city outside the window.

"Fuck you," I cannot hold it back any longer, "I was leaving."

His eyes continue to meander over me, and it is quite apparent that he is trying to figure me out. To figure out what neat little personality box I fit in.

We drive further than I have ever been. The city now outside my window looks nothing like the one I grew up in. I almost feel like I am driving into the Capitol in the Hunger Games. Everything is lush and green, nothing like the vast dirty concrete of my neighborhood.

The car slows as we pull up to a black iron gate. Luca presses a button on his visor and it slowly swings open before we drive through. Two large men in suits, both holding rather large guns, are standing along the driveway as we pass through the gate. I quickly spot two more over by the trees as we continue to drive towards the largest home I have ever seen. I cannot see them clearly, but I am sure they have guns too.

As the car pulls up to the house, I notice two more men in suits standing by the front door. These guys both have large guns resting on their hips.

Fuck. Getting away might not be as easy as I had hoped.

Luca parks the car at the stairs coming from the front door. Turning to the backseat, "You got her? Or do you want a hand?"

"I got her," Renzo says, as he climbs out of and walks around the car.

The door on my side of the car opens, and he reaches over me. His hand grazes across the shirt hugging my stomach before he unbuckles my seatbelt. I glare back at him when he stands up and gestures for me to get out of the car.

"Do I need to carry you? Or are you going to be behave?"

Swinging my legs out of the door, I stand next to the car. Renzo reaches into the backseat to grab my bag, and without thinking I push away from the car.

It's now or never.

Two steps. I make it two fucking steps before I feel his large hand wrap around my wrist and yank me backwards. My back crashes into the side of the car and a painful grunt rises from my chest. Renzo stands in front of me and takes a step towards me. I have nowhere to go as he uses his body to press me against the car.

"It appears you don't like to do as you are told."

I scoff at his words, as his fingers trail down my jaw before grabbing my chin and forcefully tilting my face up to his. My heart is currently thumping in my chest as he firmly wedges me between his body and the car.

"You can behave," his words as dark as the look in his eyes, "or I can teach you how to behave."

"You can try," I retort back, "Frank has been trying to keep me in line for years."

He releases my chin, and I stop breathing as his hands roughly trail down my torso until they reach my waist.

"I'm certain that my methods are quite different from Frank's," his words deep as I am thrown over his shoulder and carried into the house.

What the fuck does that even mean?

Chapter Nine

LORENZO

As intriguing as I find her, she is fucking infuriating.

One hand on her ass slung over my shoulder and the other holding her bag, I carry Ava into the house. Fighting to free herself from my grip, her fists pound on my back as she yells to be put down. She is strong for being such a petite thing, but she is no match for me.

With ease, I carry her up the stairs and down the hallway. Passing the rooms normally reserved for our guests, I take her all the way to the end of the hall. Opening the door across the hall from mine, I carry her into the room before dropping her bag and kicking the door shut with my foot.

She has stopped screaming and her body is obviously fatigued, but she continues to slowly pound her heavy fists against my back as I carry her towards the bed. Tossing her off my shoulder, her body splays out on the bed momentarily before she rolls and scrambles to the floor, putting the bed between us as a buffer.

Once standing, she plunges her hand into the front pocket of her shorts, pulling out a boy scout sized pocket knife. Flipping it open, she waves it in my direction.

Her eyes are a mixture of fury and fear, "Do not fucking touch me."

Actually offended by her accusation, I feel my eyes narrow and my brow furrow.

"Don't flatter yourself," I turn towards the door, "I am not the kind of man that takes it."

Opening the door, "I am the kind of man that gets begged *for* it."

My words are a deep whisper when I turn back to face her, "And then begged to stop when they can no longer take the pleasure."

Her mouth gapes at my words, and for moment I think about what it would be like to fill that filthy mouth of hers. The things I could make her do with those pouty pink lips.

Fuck.

"This is your room," my words gruff, "until I figure out what it is I am going to do with you."

Storming into the hallway, I pull the door shut with a slam behind me before crossing the hall and entering my own room. Slamming that door behind me as well, my hand is immediately grabbing my hard cock through my pants.

Fuck! This is not like me.

In this moment, I am not in control of myself. My thoughts are consumed...her soft, pale skin in the palm of my hand and how easily I could mark her...the way her breath stops when I get too close and how I could be the one to withhold it from her...her perky round ass cheek being enveloped by my hand as I repeated strike her with my palm.

And that fucking mouth.

Constantly spewing sass and filth, I want to fill it to shut her up. Yet it is so fucking beautiful. Those pouty pink lips would be gorgeous sliding up and down my cock as I fuck her throat. My hand wrapped so tightly around her neck; I can almost feel my cock through her flesh.

Unbuttoning my pants, I lean against the door and pull out my throbbing cock. Violently spitting in my hand and widening my stance, my hand firmly wraps around my cock, and I quickly spread my saliva up and down my shaft.

My breathing is rapid as I continue to stroke my hand along my length. My hips flex to meet my strokes while I dream about slamming my cock down her throat. My hands firmly fisting her hair, while I fuck her throat so hard and fast that she can barely breath. Her hands bound behind her back as she willingly lets me thoroughly use her.

A groan grows deep in my chest and sweat is glistening on my forearm, as I continue to slam my cock in and out of my fist. Knowing it is no comparison to that pretty little mouth of hers, I continue pumping towards my release.

"Fuck," I growl.

My hips sputter as my cum spills across my hand, but all I can see is Ava eagerly swallowing every drop of me. Savoring it all.

Releasing my softening cock from my tight grip, I pull off my pants and shirt while walking towards the bathroom to clean up in the shower.

My words to her were not a lie. I would never take her unwillingly. That might do it for some men, but I want my women to give me control of them.

"What the fuck am I going to do with her?" I mumble to myself, knowing I cannot keep her. Especially if I cannot figure out how to be in control of myself around her.

The real question though, is what the fuck don't I want to do with her?

Chapter Ten

AVALIE

My eyelids flutter when the sunlight hits my face. Stretching as I wake up, my body is stiff. When the realization of where I am hits me, I push my body off the floor and wedge my back against the wall.

I spent the night huddled in the corner behind the door. The little pocket knife in my hand, ready to defend myself if necessary – but I was left alone. Completely alone, except for someone sneaking in and placing a book and protein bar inside the door while I slept.

At some point I must have gotten tired and fallen asleep. I hear a door shut before footsteps travel across the hallway to my door. Renzo knocks and yells through the door, "Breakfast!"

"Fuck off, asshole," I shout back, hoping he does not barge through the door.

"Suit yourself," he grumbles. The sound of his footsteps fading as he walks down the hallway.

This little corner quickly becomes the only place in this room I use, other than the attached bathroom. I sit here all day and night, trying my hardest not to sleep. Terrified to leave myself vulnerable to these people.

Days pass and I am left alone, except for the morning and evening knocks from Renzo calling me for food. Maybe I would be more motivated to leave this room if someone did not keep sneaking food in here when I was sleeping.

My body is now sore from spending the last few nights on the hardwood floor.

Sitting in my spot, I have been planning and plotting my escape for the past two days – or more correctly how I ridiculously plan to use the pocket knife to ward off an entire mob family and get my freedom.

A gentle knock comes from the door. This is the first time he has come to my room in the middle of the day, and I am not prepared. There is slight jiggle of the handle on the door. My eyes fixated on the handle, I wait for it to turn and him to barge in. Instead, there is another gentle, quiet knock on the door. My hand slaps over my mouth in attempt to keep myself quiet, while my other trembling hand squeezes tightly around the small handle of the knife.

No matter how many times I planned this in my head, this is fucking terrifying.

The knob begins to turn, and with every millimeter it moves my heart rate increases ten-fold. As the door opens, my body presses against the wall. Ready to pounce, just waiting for my moment.

Renzo slowly steps into the room. Even with the door blocking my view, the distinct scent of that expensive woodsy cologne would give him away.

"I'm not asking this time Ava. I will carry your ass downstairs and force you to eat."

When his body clears the door, I quietly lunge towards him. Catching him off-guard, his body presses into the wall as I fall against him. I am surprised at myself as I bring the knife up to his neck.

Standing on my toes, I press the blade just below his Adam's apple. He is eerily calm as I press hard enough that the blade dimples his skin.

"I am going to leave," I continue, trying not to let him hear the fear in my voice, "and you are going to fucking let me go."

My words are the first thing to elicit a response from him – a slight smirk at the corner of his mouth.

A fucking smirk? Apparently, I am not nearly as intimidating as I thought I was.

"Unfortunately, *piccola pesca*," his words a deep gravelly whisper as his face bends down towards me, "you were sold to the Botticellis to pay a debt."

Continuing to lean forward, his weight presses the knife hard enough against his flesh that a drop of blood pools on the surface of the blade. Unfazed, he continues bending towards my face, the pool of blood now trickling down his neck and staining the collar of his shirt.

Startled at the sight, I decrease my pressure against him. As I do, his hands are on my wrists and my body is abruptly spinning towards the wall. An involuntary grunt comes from my throat when my body is slammed against it.

Renzo uses his grip on my wrists to firmly press my arms into the wall high above my head – high enough that I am still standing on my toes – as he plucks the knife from my hand. Lifting my wrists, stretching my body so painfully hard I am unable to fight back, he bends down until his face is nearly touching mine.

My breaths are loud and my chest is heaving as fear courses my body, worried about what he is going to do to me.

Firmly gripping both of my wrists in one of his hands, he continues to lift, painfully stretching me further.

My body tenses when I feel my own blade pressed against my neck.

"You belong to me," his words a dark whisper, as the tip of the knife slowly drags down my neck. The pressure is not enough to cut through my skin, but it is hard enough to feel as though he is scratching me.

"I was planning to pass you on and put you to work for my family," his eyes pass over my body, "but I believe I will keep you."

The tip of the blade continues to trail down my sternum.

"I own you," his words slow as the blade delicately crosses over the top of my now heaving breast.

What I am feeling...

"I decide what you do," his lips graze over my cheek while the tip of the blade glides around my breast to my stomach.

It isn't all fear...

"I tell you when," the blade leaves my body and I hear it click as it is folded shut.

"And I determine how," his swords a faint whisper as his lips skim my ear, erupting goosebumps on the back of my neck.

He gently presses the knife into the pocket of my shorts, before reaching towards the trickle of blood on his neck. His body firmly presses into mine as he swipes his blood-tinged thumb slowly over my lower lip, painting it red.

"You are mine," he grazes his lips over mine, pressing his firm cock against my hip, causing my pussy to clench. He releases the grip on my wrists and steps back from me, and my eyes travel to his blood-tinged lips.

"I am going to change my shirt," he says reaching for the door knob, "I expect you waiting in the hallway by the time I am done."

The door shuts and my fingers are immediately on my parted lips. My heart still racing as I feel for the flutter of his lips while rubbing his blood from me.

I cannot catch my breath or get my heart to stop beating in my throat.

He fucking terrifies me, yet I have never been so turned on and needy in my life.

Chapter Eleven

LORENZO

Closing the door to Ava's room, I stand in the hallway and stare down at my cock painfully throbbing against my pants.

She fears me, but there is no denying the sweet smell of arousal coming from her body as I pinned her against the wall and drug the knife over her flesh.

Fear and pain arouse her, and that makes me fucking hard as hell for her.

Having spent a good portion of last night deciding what to do with her, I was fully prepared to turn her over to the syndicate this morning. A pretty girl like her, she would probably wind-up serving drinks at one of our casinos – not a terrible life.

Undoing the buttons, I remove my shirt as I walk towards the bathroom. Reaching the mirror, my eyes scan down my neck. It is apparent that the cut on my neck is not deep. The knife barely felt sharp enough to break the skin. Cleaning the area, I notice that it is hardly a scratch and it has already stopped bleeding.

The eyes of the man staring back at me from the mirror do not look like my own. They have an excitement flickering in them that mine normally do not. The man on the other side is fighting the animal inside of him for control. That is not me.

I live my life as a man in complete fucking control. I am cold, cunning, and calculated in everything I do. The things I do for this family are planned out like a game of chess – knowing my next moves well in advance. My kills are precise – my message clear to our enemies. When I fuck it is cold, brutal and savage – inflicting pain and pleasure together until it is nearly unbearable for us both.

Yet, with all my planning, I never saw her coming.

I did not plan on her. I could not plan for someone like her.

She is wild. She does not listen. She talks back. She is unpredictable. She is the opposite of any woman I have ever had in my life. Her ability to make me lose control of myself is unnerving. The mere presence of her shatters my control.

Walking into my closet to grab a new shirt, I solidify my decision.

I am going to fucking keeping her. At least for now.

She will be fun to play with, and I am quite certain that she wants to play.

Crossing the room while unbuttoning my shirt, I head into the hallway to collect Ava. If she is going to be staying, she might as well get acquainted with her new home and eventually the people that are in it.

Turning the knob and pulling open my door, I am greeted by an empty hallway. No Ava.

She might make me feel, but she definitely fucking infuriates me more.

Quickly, I cross the hall and push open the door to her room. Ava is on the bed, her arms and legs crossed, staring up the ceiling.

"I thought I told you to be in the hallway," my words tinged with anger.

"No," she lifts an eyebrow and continues as her words drip with sass, "You told me you expect me to be in the hallway."

"Up," I demand, stalking towards the bed.

"I'd rather not," she quips back, "You should learn now that I am going to be a difficult hostage."

Towering over her, I repeat my command, "Up."

She pisses me off.

She rolls her eyes at me and then continues staring at the ceiling.

Fuck!

My cock twitches in my pants at the thought of making her eyes roll with my touch.

"You might be difficult," my words sharp as I lean towards the bed.

Grabbing her by the wrists, I pull her from the bed and throw her body over my shoulder.

"...but there will be punishment for failing to do as you are told."

Before she has an opportunity to retort my statement, my palm quickly and firmly strikes her ass with two rapid slaps.

A pleasantly surprising raspy groan pushes from her throat before she swings her fists at my back and yells, "Put me down, asshole!"

Turning to leave the room, I place my hand on her ass to hold her in place. Giving a firm squeeze to the cheek that took my assault, I carry her from the room and down the hall.

She is going to take my punishments so fucking well, for which she we be well rewarded.

Licking my lips at the thought, we head downstairs with her still draped over my shoulder. Reaching the bottom, I pause.

"If I put you down, are you going to behave?"

"Fine," her response bratty and childish.

Thoughts of spanking her perky, round ass one more time cross my mind before placing her feet on the floor.

"If you are going to be staying here a while-"

"What makes you think I'm staying?" she interrupts me.

Reaching out, my fingers wrap around her delicate throat. As much as I want to, I do not squeeze. At least not this time.

"I own you," my words deep and slow as I use my grip to angle her face up to mine, "and I say you are staying."

Releasing her, I begin to walk in the direction of the kitchen. My words smug, "Also, the guards outside have been instructed to shoot to kill if you try to leave."

She lets out a loud huff and the pad of her feet tells me that she has begun to follow behind me, eliciting a small smirk on my face – one I am happy she is not able to see from behind my back.

"You are welcome almost anywhere in the house," I turn to look at her.

Pausing to point at my father's office, "Except in there. That room is off-limits. Listen to me on this one, *piccola pesca*, because even I might not be able to protect you from the wrath of my father."

Her eyes widen a little, before she nods, acknowledging that she understands.

"While we are at it," I turn and continue walking, "it is also probably in your best interest to stay out of V's room."

"Who is V?" she quietly questions.

"Venecia," I reply entering the kitchen, "my sister."

"You mean your whole family lives here?"

"Yes," my answer abrupt.

"Aren't you a little old to still live at home?"

Turning to face her yet again, I am unable to read the expression on her face, but I am certain she is trying to see just how far she can push me.

"Obviously, this is the kitchen. The staff serve both breakfast and dinner at seven. If you need something outside of that, help yourself to whatever you want.

Except the knives, I suggest you leave those in the drawer."

Abruptly turning, I walk past her and head down the hall. I can hear her walking quickly behind me, the strides of her shorter legs struggling to keep up with my pace.

After showing her various rooms on the main floor, I push open the double doors to the library.

Chapter Twelve

AVALIE

Speed walking, I am trying to keep up with Renzo as he shows me around the house. Right now, I am just trying to keep track of where everything is that he is showing me. I will mentally try to unpack the fact that I am being held captive here, yet I have free reign to do almost anything I want, later.

Renzo stops in front of a set of wooden double doors, before pushing them both open. Stepping inside behind him, I am in awe of the room that stands before me.

The walls to my left and right are floor to ceiling shelves, lined with books. Stepping further inside and slowly turning, the shelves also fully span the wall behind me. The sun is shining through the wall of windows directly across from me. Through those windows is a lush, colorful garden.

If I am going to be held captive, at least I can pretend to be Belle until I figure out how to get the hell out of here.

"I see you like it in here," Renzo interrupts my thoughts, his voice almost sounds warm...and inviting.

Shit! Was I smiling?

"You are also permitted to walk in the garden," his voice immediately back to deep and cold, "The guards will leave you alone out there."

Scanning the title of the books along the right wall, I hear Renzo walking towards the door. Leaving the books behind, I jog to catch up with him.

"You can stay," he says when he hears me jogging to catch up with him.

He stops, turning to face me and I almost crash into him. Looking up, I am so mesmerized with the golden flakes of his hazel eyes that I barely comprehend what he says next.

"Make yourself at home. My family is aware that you are here. I will be leaving for work until much later tonight," he stares into my eyes as though he is trying to read my mind, "Do not let me hear that you were a nuisance when I return."

Just this once, I am going to do as I am told, at least in regards to staying in the library. Heading back inside, my fingers dance across the various book spines as I pull a few to take back to my room. *Pride and Prejudice. The Bridges of Madison County. The Princess Bride.* This room is full of lots of love stories for a ruthless crime family.

Juggling the books in one hand, I pull the doors shut to the library before heading back upstairs to my...

Captive's Suite?

I can't exactly call it a prison. The bedroom and attached bath are nearly the size of the apartment that I grew up in. The mattress is soft and feels like what I would imagine floating on a cloud would be like. The linens on the bed feel luxurious. I am actually looking forward to curling up on the bed to read.

Days of weird civility pass as I co-exist in this house with Renzo. He forces me to join him for breakfast and dinner, ensuring that I am eating. Conversations are minimal, but amicable – like neighbors making small talk. Outside of meals, he stays away from me. It is almost as though he is making an effort not to be around me.

Being left alone, I spend most of my days wandering this massive house and perusing the titles in the library. At the rate I am going, I will have read the whole library by the end of the month.

Returning to my room from yet another trip down to the library for new books, I hear a noise behind me. Turning around, the door to Renzo's room is open and he is standing with his back to me. Every inch of him previously covered in stuffy dress shirts is decorated with tattoos. A massive, realistic looking lion roars across the rippled muscles of his shoulders and back. The detail of the tattoos covering his body is astounding. I have never seen a man built like him before – at least not in person.

An involuntary gasp comes from my mouth, causing him to turn around. The front of him covered in more black ink, accentuating the ripples of his abs and those muscles on his hips that point directly to his crotch.

The corner of his mouth turns up at the sight of me.

Shit! He knows I was gawking at him.

Why the fuck am I staring at the guy who is holding me captive against my will? The man who actually believes he owns me.

Because he's fucking hot, Ava. That's why.

Renzo quickly crosses the distance to the door. Watching him as his eyes scan over my body, for once in my life I am at a loss for words.

"We don't spy on people in this house," his words angry as the door slams shut in my face causing me to startle and drop the books from my hand.

Picking up the books, I struggle to hold them as I fidget with the doorknob to my room. Finally getting it to turn, I hastily enter the room, shutting the door behind me before flopping on the bed.

I read through the first chapter of *The Godfather*, rereading several paragraphs because I am unable to concentrate. I feel the urge to apologize. Well, not apologize, but tell him that I was not spying.

Why the fuck do I even care?

Standing with my hand on the doorknob for a moment, I try to figure out what it is that I am going to say to him. Opening my door, I am surprised to find that his door is open again. Crossing the hallway, I stop at his doorway to knock.

When there is no answer, I call out, "Renzo?"

Still no answer, I step through the threshold into his room.

You shouldn't be in here.

He has told me numerous times to make myself at home, and that is what I am doing.

No, you're snooping – spying. The thing he literally just yelled about.

Looking around at his room, it is impeccably tidy. Everything has a place and is in order. Peering into the closet, everything is neatly hung or folded, and arranged by both clothing type and color. Opening the drawers to the dresser, even his boxer briefs are neatly rolled and arranged by color.

Control freak, much?

Unable to control myself, my hands are in the drawer tossing things around. When finished, it looks like they were all dumped in the drawer. Smugly content with myself, I push the drawer shut and head back into the bedroom. My eyes are drawn to a large armoire to the left of the bed.

With a closet that big, who needs an armoire?

Ensuring I wrinkle the hotel-perfect linens, I crawl across the four-poster bed to look inside the armoire. My hand rests on the knob for a moment, instinct telling me I should not look inside.

He told you to make yourself at home...

Curiosity gets the better of me. Pulling open the door, my mouth falls open. In front of me are neatly hung ropes, leather cuffs, various wooden paddles, and other items. I try to imagine what they might be for.

The door behind me slams and the studded leather handcuffs I was holding drop to the floor.

The words blurt from my mouth as I pick up the cuffs and spin around to find a very angry looking Renzo, "I...uh...I came to tell you that I wasn't spying on you."

His eyes fixed on mine, he walks towards me without saying a word. Taking the cuffs from my hand, he places them back on their hook and closes the armoire door.

"Out," he quietly commands.

Surprised by his calm reaction my feet ignore my brain, and I am frozen in place with my heart pounding in my chest.

Chapter Thirteen

LORENZO

"Ava," I loom over her, "Get out. I cannot be held responsible for what happens if you stay."

Her eyes are wide, I am sure in response to what looks like pure anger on my face. I am not angry she is in here, but I am struggling to control myself with her behind this closed door.

"What are you going to do, kill me?" sarcasm oozes on every word, as though she is unaware of just how easily I could actually end her life.

Stepping closer to her, my nostrils are flaring as my fingers wrap around her throat.

"Go ahead and do it," she wraps her hand over top of mine and squeezes. Urging me, "End my miserable, pathetic life."

Squeezing tighter, I can feel her pulse throbbing against my fingers. Using my grip and leverage, I force her to walk backwards until her back is flush with the post at the foot of the bed. She has nowhere to go as I continue to inch closer to her, yet she does not cower.

"I am not going to kill you," her eyes widen at my words, "but I am going to punish you for continuing to disobey me."

Releasing her neck and grabbing her wrists, I pull them both over her head and press them against the post. Clicking a handcuff around her wrist, her eyes dart up to her hands and widen a little when she sees a second cuff dangling from a hook in the post above her head.

No screams or fighting, as I pull her onto her toes to clasp the second cuff around her wrist.

Stepping back, I admire the position she is in. The height of the cuffs coupled with her short stature has her balancing on her toes to keep herself from dangling from the chains restraining her. Her petite frame is stretched tight, fighting to maintain her footing.

"You've made your point, asshole!"

"Oh, *piccola pesca*," I unbutton my shirt cuffs and meticulously roll up my sleeves while slowly walking back towards her, "I have not even come close to making my point."

Reaching her, I slide my hand into the front pocket of her shorts and am pleased when I find the pocket knife. Her rapid breathing stops for a second when I flip it open and move it towards her neck. Grabbing the neckline of her shirt, I pull it away from her body before slicing the knife through the light fabric to the hem.

As it falls open, I am greeted with a sheer, pink, lace bra and round, heaving breasts. Not a sound comes from her, except her heavy breathing, as I cut the shirt from her body.

"You aren't afraid of me?" I question as I dip my fingers into the top of her shorts and unbutton them.

"Why should I be?" the expression on her face firm and cold, "you already said you aren't going to rape me or kill me."

"That doesn't mean I am not going to hurt you."

"You wouldn't be the first."

Unzipping her shorts, I push them over her hips until they fall to her feet. I am pleased to find her thong is the same sheer lace as her bra, nearly granting me full view of her shaved cunt.

Her body is fucking perfection, and I am going to teach her just what it is capable of.

Returning to the armoire, I pull open the door to browse the contents. My eyes are immediately drawn to a large red leather crop. Sliding my fingers around the handle, my cock twitches at the idea of leaving beautiful red marks across her skin with it.

Her face is still brave as I walk towards her, gently flicking the crop against the palm of my hand.

"Don't you dare fucking hit me with that," her eyes narrow at me.

"I told you I have ways of teaching you to behave," I flick the crop hard against my palm. The firm, red leather thuds against my skin with a slight sting, "and there will be punishments for continuously disobeying me."

Placing the crop just below her chin, I slowly drag it down her neck allowing her the opportunity to feel it against her skin. Her breaths are fast and shallow, causing her chest to quiver with each inhale. Her blue eyes locked on mine as the crop traces between her cleavage and down her stomach, leaving a trail of goosebumps in its wake.

Continuing, I drag the crop from her navel to the delicate lace of her thong, gliding it over her and between her thighs. Grabbing her hip, I spin her around, eliciting a loud gasp as she struggles to keep her balance on her toes.

Her face and chest against the bedpost, bound like this her back is arched, pushing her beautiful round ass cheeks towards me.

"This is a crop, and it is going to sting," I say as I gently place the crop against her right cheek.

"Don't you da-," her words cut short by one firm strike where I was resting the crop. A mixture of a groan and yelp rise from her chest, as her body quickly reacts to sensation.

Chapter Fourteen

AVALIE

The leather strikes my ass and my whole body tightens, causing me to struggle to stay on my toes. A noise of pure pleasure and pain rises from my chest and fills the room.

I feel him step close, until he is pressed against my back. His lips graze my neck as he presses them to my ear.

"I can use pain to hurt you, *piccola pesca*. To punish you," his words a deep whisper, sending chills through my body, "but done right, pain can bring you more pleasure than you've ever known."

His teeth scrape down my neck and I pull away. The leather strikes my cheek again...and again. My head falls back, a breathy moan erupting from my lungs.

Renzo gently rubs his fingers over my red sensitive flesh, "Your skin marks so beautifully."

"Is that all you've got?" My voice trembles back at him as I rest my face against the bed post.

I refuse to let him win.

He groans back at me as he strikes me again. I cry out, the vibrations of his hit traveling straight to my center. The sting shoots through my body causing me to lose my balance and slip from my toes. I expect to fall and hang from my restraints, but Renzo's arm wraps around my waist, holding me until I steady myself back on my toes.

"You like the pain," his words slow and hungry as he turns me to face him.

"Fuck you," my words raspy, "I don't."

His fingers travel down my side, feeling like fire on my skin. Passing over my hip, he dips his hand between my thighs.

"Deny it all you want, *piccola pesca*," he slowly pulls his hand back, "but your sweet pussy is fucking soaked."

His eyes locked on mine, he slowly licks each of his fingers as though he is savoring the taste of me.

"You are so fucking wet, it's dripping down your thighs."

He isn't wrong. My pussy is wet and has never felt so needy.

The leather in his hand gently flicks against my panties, and it feels like every nerve in my clit fires at once.

"Fuck...," trembles from my lips in a breathy moan.

Slapping against my panties again, my thighs tremble as he hooks a finger under my thong pulling it to the side – fully exposing me to him.

"If you don't want this," he steps closer until his body is flush against mine and whispers, "you need to tell me to stop now."

My mouth opens, but not a sound passes over my parted lips. This is my opportunity to end whatever this is...

But I don't think I want this to stop.

His eyes glimmer with a hint of surprise, as though he was fully expecting me to tell him to stop.

I gasp as the smooth, wooden handle of the crop slides between my folds, gently passing over my clit as Renzo drags it to my opening.

"I'm just getting it wet for you," his words as slow as the handle sliding flush through the folds of my pussy again, my whole body trembling at his touch.

Wrapping his arm around my waist and pulling my body towards his chest, his nostrils flare as he slowly slides the handle inside of me. The foreign sensation causes my knees to buckle, dropping my hips further onto the handle causing me to groan as it plunges inside of me and rubs along my walls.

Renzo's thrusts with the handle are steady, slowly pulling it nearly from me and quickly thrusting it back inside. My body was already wound so tight, that I am on the verge of coming.

Arching my back, I open my hips allowing him better access to me and he quickly takes advantage. The thrusts and pulls now both fast as he works the handle in and out of me. My body trembling as I quickly approach my release.

"Pain is pleasure, *piccola pesca*," he whispers as his mouth kisses down my neck to my shoulder.

"Now listen for once, and come for me like a good fucking girl," he firmly slaps my ass before changing the angle of the thrusting handle.

My orgasm explodes through my body like a fucking bomb, shattering me to pieces. Screams of pleasure erupt from me, as my pussy clenches around the handle continuing to thrust into me. My body writhing in Renzo's hold, as he continues to work the handle in and out of my body. Repeated orgasms consume my body until things slowly go black.

My eyelids flutter, and when I open them I find myself lying in my bed under the covers. I am naked, exhausted, and my whole body is sore.

Shit. Was that a fucking dream?

Climbing from bed and walking into the bathroom, I am surprised to find the tub filled with steamy water and bubbles. On the edge of the tub is a note and a tube of lotion. Picking them both up, I turn towards the sink and take in my disheveled appearance.

"That fucking asshole," I yell to myself in the mirror upon seeing the bruised bite mark on my shoulder.

Not a fucking dream...

He fucking shackled me and assaulted me...

I didn't say yes...

...but I didn't say 'no,' even when he offered to stop.

I didn't want...to say 'no.'

I didn't fight.

I fucking parted my thighs so he could go deeper.

Even now, the thought of the leather cracking against my skin gives me goosebumps.

What the fuck, Ava?

Stretching my sore body, I read the note:

> Take the bath, your body needs it. Use
> the cream on my marks, it will help.
> Behave while I am gone, or I will be

forced to punish you again when I return.
-Lorenzo

"No fucking chance," I mumble to myself. That shouldn't have happened, and definitely will not happen again.

As much as I do not want to do a thing he says, every inch of my body hurts and the idea of a bath sounds amazing. Dipping my toe in, I test the water before slowly sliding my body into the massive tub.

I'll never tell him he was right, but this feels fucking fantastic.

Chapter Fifteen

LORENZO

Holding Ava as she comes undone repeatedly in my arms, is playing on repeat in my mind. When it does stop, I am envisioning all the things that I want to do with her body. Fucking her with my hard cock until she cannot take any more pleasure.

Walking into a meeting with Dmitriy Andreyev is not the time to be distracted. With Luca and Antonio following behind me, we walk towards the club. Approaching the back door, two men step from the building towards us.

"I am here to see Dmitriy," addressing them as we continue to approach, "He is expecting me."

Pulling his suit jacket to the side to reveal the gun tucked into his waistband, the bigger of the two responds in a thick Russian accent, "Stop. We need to check you before you can go inside."

Spreading my feet and lifting my arms, I prepare to be patted down and searched for weapons. Expecting this, I had handed mine to Luca before we entered the alley. Luca and Antonio are still carrying and ready to use if necessary.

The smaller guy approaches and searches me before nodding to the larger guy. He did such a shitty job that I could have snuck a small arsenal inside with me.

"They stay here," the big guy gestures towards my guys before turning back to me, "You follow me."

"Five minutes," I look towards Luca, trusting that if I do not walk out of this building, he will come in shooting.

Passing through the kitchen, I follow the large Russian up a flight of stairs to an office that overlooks the club below. Standing at the window is Dmitriy Andreyev, second in command to the Andreyev Family.

He is a tall, lanky man just a year older than me – also taking over his father's business. In our youth, our families were at peace with one another, and we were actually friends. Now, all of the families are at war, fighting to obtain total control of the city, and we have become cordial enemies.

"Lorenzo," he walks towards me extending his hand, "my old friend."

Taking his hand in mine, I shake it, "Dmitriy."

"What is so important that you needed to come down here to see me in person?"

"I am sure you have heard of the string of arsons currently affecting our businesses," I say flatly sitting into a chair by the window.

"Yes," he sits, "I have heard your family was having some difficulties and struggling right now."

"No difficulties," my words firm, quickly denouncing any perceived weaknesses he may have about the Botticellis, "I wanted to look in your eyes when I asked if you knew which of the families was behind it."

"You mean if the Andreyev's are behind it," he scoffs.

"If you are," my words direct, "you know what that means."

"Lorenzo," Dmitriy pauses, "we are old friends."

"Old friends, Dmitriy. Not current friends," I stand from my chair and walk towards the door, "I trust, as an old friend, you will let me know if you hear anything."

"Of course, my friend," he responds, as I exit the office and head back down the stairs. Passing through the door at the rear of the kitchen, I walk towards Luca and Antonio.

"We can go," I say as Luca hands me back my gun and we head back towards the car. Reaching the car, I climb into the passenger seat, Luca to the driver, and Antonio in the back.

"Is it them?" Luca questions as he starts the car.

"He didn't deny it," I reply as Luca pulls away from the alley, "but I don't think it was him. He's always been such an arrogant ass, that he would not have been able to deny it. He also didn't try to kill me."

Earlier today I arranged similar meetings with important members of the Armenian, Triad, and Yakusa families as well. If someone is going to come for us, they are going to know that we are not afraid to step foot on their turf either.

"Where to?" Luca questions.

"Head to the Armenians'," I instruct him, "Levon is expecting us shortly."

The meetings with each family do not go much differently than my meeting with Dmitriy. Whoever is coming for us, is doing a good job keeping it quiet.

The sun is rising by the time I walk out of my meeting with the Triad. Having a full day of business to tend to, and knowing we will not be heading home until sunset, the boys and I head to the Fourth Street Diner for some coffee and breakfast.

Chapter Sixteen

AVALIE

Until I manage to find a way out of here, I refuse to live like a captive or a hostage. Renzo told me I could make myself at home, and that is exactly how I have spent my day.

I made myself a late breakfast in the kitchen, since I slept well past seven. After cleaning everything up, I wandered through the house and made myself familiar with all of the rooms that Renzo had not shown me. Actually listening for once, I stayed clear of his father's office. All these days in this huge house, and I have yet to run into a single person that is not hired help. It is strange, considering it is quite obvious by the state of the bedrooms in this house that several people live here.

Having walked to and from the produce store at least once a day for most of my life, I miss being outside. It's a sunny day, so I decide to take advantage and check out the garden while getting in a few steps. My leisurely stroll was quite enjoyable, and I found a great little spot to lay and read for a bit. It felt amazing to be outside in the sun again – even if I was being watched by armed guards the entire time.

Passing through the library, I stop to grab another book before heading upstairs. Since I cannot seem to rid myself of thoughts of Renzo's hands aggressively combing over my body, I opt for Stephen King over romance this time.

Maybe if I scare the shit of myself, I'll stop thinking about those mind-blowing orgasms for more than five minutes.

Reaching my room, I look at the clock and realize it's already six. After laying out in the sun most of the afternoon, I should probably take a shower before dinner. Giving myself a quick sniff, I realize just how needed that shower is.

Stripping off my clothes, I head to the bathroom and turn on the shower. While waiting for the water to warm, my eyes catch a glimpse of the nearly faded bite mark on my shoulder. My pussy clenches at the thought of his hands on my body while his teeth bite through my flesh.

Fuck. This is so wrong.

Standing in the bathroom getting wet over the man who basically bought me and fantasizing about him having his way with me, I start to realize that I might be a little fucked up.

Just a little fucked up?

He is unbelievably hot, and that was literally the most amazing orgasm of my life – and the first ever from a man. There is no harm in using him as inspiration for a little self-care.

Keep telling yourself that, Ava.

Stepping into the shower, the hot water sprays over my body from the rain head in the ceiling. Closing my eyes and imaging his hands running down my body, I part my thighs and press my hand between them. My fingers immediately dancing over and around my clit.

Fuck, the thought of him taking me is hot.

My breathing is rapid when my fingers plunge inside me. Biting my lip, I try to hold back my moan.

"And what are you doing?" Renzo's inquisitive voice scares me nearly to death.

"Fuck! Get out, asshole," I yell back at him attempting to cover myself with my hands.

He does not leave. Instead, he leans against the wall opposite the shower, crosses his arms, and repeats his question, "What are you doing?"

"You know damned well what I was doing! Now get out!"

"Did I give you permission to come?"

"Did you what?" his question catches me off-guard.

"You belong to me," his voice deep and gravelly, "I decide when you come."

"I'm sorry, but the fuck you do," my hand dips back between my thighs.

He might've provided the greatest orgasm of all time, but I'll be damned if he thinks he actually owns me. That he can control me. He will never control me.

"Are you sure you want to test me?" Renzo pulls open the glass door and stands fully clothed at the edge of the shower.

Ignoring his question, I close my eyes. Determined to prove him wrong, that he does not own me, my fingers vigorously rub my clit.

"You want to play?" his voice menacing as he firmly grabs my chin, "we can play."

"Eyes on me," he demands, "show me what it is you *think* you like."

His grip squeezes on my chin and I open my eyes, immediately met with his staring back at me. The hazel of his eyes looks nearly golden, like there is actually fire burning in them as they slowly scan up and down my body.

"It's not enough," his hand slides from my chin to my throat, "is it, *piccola pesca?*"

His fingers tighten, squeezing my throat and restricting my ability to breathe.

"Your body now knows how good pain makes your pleasure feel. And it needs it," his grip tightens more, "I can feel your heart beating faster at just the thought of it."

Maintaining eye contact with him, I plunge two fingers deep inside of me. Curling them, I stroke against that spot that normally does me in.

Fuck. He's fucking right.

"You know I'm right," he whispers, releasing my throat.

Panting, the need to come is painful, but I cannot get there.

"You like how good the pain feels," his hand strokes down my chest.

His finger flicks my tight nipple, and I let out a whimper as the sensation shoots straight to my clit.

"You fucking need it," he flicks me again, "Give yourself what you need."

Using my free hand, I roll my nipple between my fingers.

"Harder," Renzo commands.

I cannot help but follow his demand. Squeezing my nipple hard, I tug on it while continuing to pump my fingers inside of me.

Staring into his eyes, I pull harder and ride my hand. I can feel the orgasm building in my core, readying to explode.

"Enough," his voice harsh.

So close to the edge, I ignore him and continue working towards my release.

"Enough, Ava," his words quickly growing angry and impatient, "I said stop."

I groan, my climax so close.

"Fuck," I scream, fumbling for the water knob, as I am suddenly showered with icy cold water.

"I told you," his voice smug, "you belong to me, and I determine when you come."

"Fucking asshole."

"There is a dress on the bed for you. We will not be alone tonight, and your shorts are not appropriate for dinner."

Other people really do live here?

"Punishment comes in many forms," he calls back as he walks from the bathroom, "I expect you downstairs promptly at seven."

Fuck, that is cruel.

Every man I have ever been with, until Renzo, has left me unsatisfied. But they have all been bumbling boys with no clue what they were doing. None of them have brought me to edge and yanked me back from the cliff like this.

It has been nearly two weeks since he chained me to his bed and whipped me with the crop. His touch in the shower is the most physically intimate he has attempted to be with me since then. There have been touches - grazes - and wandering eyes. But not once has he tried to really touch me.

My body is so fucking needy, and I want what only he can give me.

I fucking need it.

Shit! Is that his plan?

He did say he would make me beg for it.

The internal argument about fucking this man is consuming me. It is nearly the only thing I think about.

It's wrong.

I know it's wrong.

But it's good…so fucking good.

If I am going to be stuck here, is it wrong to allow myself the indulgence of this gorgeous man pleasuring me?

It's just sex.

He thinks owns me.

I'll let him use my body, because I do enjoy what I get from it in return. But my body is all he will own of me.

Chapter Seventeen

LORENZO

"Punishment comes in many forms," I call back to her as I walk from the bathroom, "I expect you downstairs promptly at seven."

I have always considered myself to be a bit of a sadist — inflicting pain on others my kink. The way skin bruises when sucked hard. Watching skin turn red from being paddled. The sensation of sinking my teeth into a woman's flesh. That is what makes sex exciting for me — what I need to make it exciting.

Until her. Until Ava. I enjoy inflicting pain and punishing her. She is different than the other women because she also thoroughly enjoys the pain. Receiving it turns her on, just like inflicting it does to me.

Yet, the pain is merely an appetizer to the joy that is the meal of her coming fucking undone. Watching her come does things to me I did not know were possible. Pleasuring her is as exciting as punishing her.

She is going to be my undoing.

Heading to my room to change out of my damp clothes, I opt to take a much-needed, quick, cold shower myself.

After dressing, I head downstairs and straight to the study to pour myself two-fingers of bourbon. Sipping on the warm liquid, I am caught off-guard at the site of Ava walking down the stairs.

The items I had laid out for her were nothing more than just a simple, flowy summer dress. Yet it is anything but simple on her. The low neck shows off just the right amount of cleavage, while the rest of the dress delicately dances along her skin, giving a subtle glimpse at the curves beneath it. Her makeup is light, but she is naturally beautiful without it. Her blonde hair is swept into a loose braid falling over her shoulder. She is absolutely stunning.

Reaching the landing, she heads straight for me.

"I'm pleased to see that not only are you on time, you are early."

Her delicate hand takes the glass of bourbon from me before downing the last of it in a single gulp.

"Spicy," she grins and hands the glass back to me, "Another?"

"I do not like my women sloppy, Ava."

"Well," her finger drags across my chest as she begins to walk towards the study, "I guess it's a good thing I'm not your woman then."

Fucking bewildered at her sudden increase in audacity, I stand in the hallway for a moment shaking my head at my now empty glass. By the time I enter the study, she has ice in a glass and is pouring herself a solid four-fingers.

Stepping flush against her back, "But you are," my words deep as I pour half of her drink into my glass before pulling her from the bar.

Rolling her eyes, she follows behind me.

Oh, piccola pesca, you will fucking pay for that.

Entering the dining room, I pull out a chair for her at the far edge of the table before sitting in the chair next to her. The rest of my family slowly enters the room, filling in from the other end of the table, the seats at our end staying empty.

Always the talkative one, V turns towards us to chat up Ava.

"You must be Ava," she smiles, "I'm Venecia, but everyone just calls me V."

"Avalie, but everyone calls me Ava," she smiles as though this is a fucking dinner party.

"I have heard a lot about you while I was away," she smiles smugly at me, "I am happy to finally meet you."

After a moment of cordial greetings from around the table, V questions, "So how did you two meet anyway?"

Just as I am about to answer, Ava does.

"Renzo took me as payment for a debt. So apparently he owns me now. Or your family does. I'm not really sure how all of this works. This mafia shit is all new to me."

"I like her Renzo," V laughs, "but you are in fucking trouble with this one."

"Venecia, fucking language at the table," my father bellows as he enters the room.

"Sorry Papa," she quickly replies with a smile, ignoring the hypocrisy of his words.

Conversation around the table quickly turns to recounts of everyone's day and casual chat as everyone begins to eat.

"You look beautiful this evening," I quietly say to Ava, "but watch yourself, because you are really testing my patience this evening."

She stabs her fork into a piece of potato on my plate, "I'm sorry, but I don't understand." Her eyes on me, she puts it into her mouth and swallows.

"Are you trying to test me? Because you do not want to play with me."

Maintaining eye contact, she takes a long, slow and savory sip of her bourbon before responding, "But maybe I do."

Fuck!

"I play by my rules," my voice quiet and firm, "Are you sure you want that?"

Ava smiles at me as she gives a single nod of her head, causing my cock to immediately begin to rise in my pants. I have managed to keep her at arm's length for nearly two weeks and now I am struggling not to bend her over this table and fuck her senseless.

Placing my hand on Ava's thigh and my lips to her ear, I whisper, "Take off your panties."

"Excuse me," she chokes around her food.

"You heard me," I repeat into her ear, "Take off your panties."

Her eyes dart around the room and then to me, "I think I'll be keeping my panties, thank you."

"You wanted to play. You agreed to my rules," I growl into her ear, "You can take them off yourself or I can take them off for you."

"You wouldn't fucking dare."

"But I would," quickly pushing my chair back from the table, all eyes turn to me as I stand up.

Ava's eyes go wide when she realizes that I have no problem separating her from her panties at this table, and she quickly nods her head at me.

"Everything is fine. I just dropped my napkin," I address everyone while sitting back into my chair.

As everyone turns their attention back to their food and previous conversations, I return mine to Ava.

"Panties. Now," I quietly demand.

After an exasperated exhale, her fingers slowly make their way under her dress, eventually pulling her panties down her thighs. Pushing them over her knees, she discreetly passes them over her feet before placing them in my waiting palm.

"Good girl," I groan quietly into her ear while shoving them into my pocket, "eventually you will learn not to make me ask you to do something twice."

Placing my hand on her thigh, I slowly slide it to her knee before yanking her leg towards me and opening her thighs. My hand grazes along her inner thigh and under her dress until I can almost feel the warmth of her pussy.

Grabbing my wrist, she pushes my hand away. In return, I pinch the thin skin of her inner thigh causing her to hiss under her breath.

"Hands on the table," I demand, "do not do that again."

Moving my hand back towards her warmth, "I expect you to be quiet. I don't want to hear a sound out of you."

She is radiating warmth against my fingers as I hold them against her, the soft skin of her warm cunt resting against my hand. Slowly parting her lips, I slide a finger between them and hear her swallow hard as I pass over top of her clit. Already so wet for me, I use her arousal to continuously glide my finger in small circles around her clit. All of my focus on that single tiny bundle of nerves, her short breaths become increasingly rapid as her fingertips flex against the table.

Her staggered breathing tells me how close she is, and I slide my hand from her slick center to her knee. I wrap my hand tightly around it to keep her thighs parted. With my free hand, I pick up my fork and continue to eat the food on my plate.

Her pending release quickly converts to frustration as I deny her what she so desperately wanted.

"You should eat," I smirk at her.

After a few minutes, Ava's breathing returns to normal. Just as it does, I swipe my fingers across her entrance before rubbing them firmly over her clit, quickly bringing her back to the brink. Watching as she silently chews on her bottom lip, I squeeze her clit between my fingers. Rolling it between them, I feel her thighs begin to quiver before letting go and returning my hand back to her knee.

Ava's body is tight. Tense. Dying for a release. The frustration she is feeling is nearly visible in her body language. I cannot get enough of how needy her body gets.

"Renzo," she begs in a whisper. Her voice so needy and desperate, for something she knows only I can give her.

"My rules," I mouth back her.

Traveling my hand back up towards her entrance, her eyelids flutter and her thighs quiver with anticipation. Without warning, I slide a finger inside of her and repeatedly curl it against her walls. Feeling her clench around my finger, her body is begging to finally come. She needs it, and I do not intend to give her. At least not yet.

As I pull my finger from her, she pulls her dress over her knees and promptly pushes her chair back from the table. All eyes are immediately on her as she stands.

Chapter Eighteen

AVALIE

Unable to take his torture anymore, I am ready to scream as I push myself from the table.

"Excuse me," I can feel my cheeks turning pink with everyone's eyes suddenly on me, "I'm suddenly not feeling well and am going to head upstairs."

Quickly leaving the dining room, I head for the stairs. Hearing footsteps behind me as I near the top, I pick up my pace.

I think I made a mistake. I can't do this with him. I just need to get to my room. Tomorrow, I will tell him it was a mistake.

I make it halfway down the hallway before two rough hands grab my shoulders, stopping me in my tracks. I am pulled backwards until I am flush against his hard body. His lips immediately trailing up my neck towards my ear.

"Where do you think you're going, *piccola pesca?*" the words a warm, gravelly whisper in my ear, "We are playing by my rules and you don't get to run from me unless I tell you to."

Nothing comes from my parted lips but continuously heavier breaths as his teeth slowly slide down my neck and he presses his hard cock against my ass.

"I think you want me to punish you," his words sending goosebumps over me, "and I intend to give you exactly what you want."

Before I have a moment to speak, Renzo turns me and pins me to the wall. His hands firmly gripping my wrists over my head and his body pressed so firmly against me I can barely breathe. Adjusting his grip to hold my wrists with just one hand, the other immediately wrapping its fingers around my throat.

"I will not give you more pain than you can handle," his words slow and dripping with lust, "but I cannot promise you the same of your pleasure."

As I gasp, his tongue plunges into my mouth. This kiss is not sweet or romantic. It is needy. Savage. Wanting. Dirty. Our tongues dance together, violent and angry.

Releasing my wrists, he mercilessly grabs my thighs to lift me around his waist before carrying me the remainder of the hallway to his room. Entering the room, he uses our bodies to close the door. The impact knocking the air from my lungs as he ends the brutal assault on my mouth. My mouth left desperately wanting more.

With sheer finesse, my feet are lowered to the ground as Renzo pulls the dress over my head, leaving me completely exposed in front of him. His tongue delectably slides across his lower lip as his belt is quickly pulled from the loops of his pants.

"Turn around," his words as savage as the look in his eyes, "hands on the door."

I know I shouldn't, but I follow his demands without hesitation. Turning to face the door, I place my palms on it as his arm wraps around my waist. In a smooth motion, he lifts me – pulling my lower body away from the door and spreading my legs. Pushing me forward, I am now bent at the waist, legs spread, with my forearms and palms resting on the door.

An animalistic growl rises from his chest as I hear him step back from me, "Fucking beautiful."

My heart thumping in my chest and both of our rapid breaths the only sounds I can hear.

"Make sure you breathe," his words quickly followed by the crack of his belt, the stinging of the flesh on my upper right thigh, and my whimper.

He growls again as the belt crashes over my left check, the impact causing my legs to tremble.

"Breathe," his voice commanding, yet comforting, as the belt strikes across my right cheek.

"You take my pain so well, *piccola pesca,*" he groans as the belt strikes my right cheek again.

Tears well in the corners of my eyes as the belt snaps twice in rapid succession across my upper thighs. My breathing is so rapid, I can hardly catch my breath, as a loud moan trembles in my throat.

Stepping closer, the belt passes in front of my face before I feel the warm leather wrap around my neck.

"Now, let's see how well you take my pleasure," the belt tightens as he steps between my legs, his hands gripping my ass, as he presses the head of his cock to my entrance. He pushes himself inside, painfully stretching me to accommodate his size.

"So fucking tight," he growls behind me, "and so fucking wet. You like the pain I give you."

Airy whimpers quiver off my lips as he pulls out and slides back into me, coating himself with my arousal. Pulling out he slams back into me, my arms bracing hard against the door while a load moan bellows from my chest.

He slowly retreats and slams into me again, as he begins to pick up his pace until he is relentlessly slapping his hips against my ass. His massive cock filling me and rubbing along every sensitive nerve with each stroke.

"Rub your clit," he growls, pulling on the belt as he continues to pound into me, "Make yourself come around my cock.

Already so close, my body is ready to explode when my fingers reach between my legs. Within seconds my orgasm is crashing through my body, my arm on the door barely able to support me as Renzo continues to savagely slide in and out of me.

"Again," he commands, standing me upright and shoving my chest against the door, "I didn't say to stop."

When I do not return my hand to my clit, he grabs it and pulls it between my thighs. Working my fingers over my clit, he continues to thrust into me so hard my body flexes onto my toes.

Breathy screams are coming from my mouth with each thrust, as our fingers are aggressively working my already over-sensitive clit. He pinches my clit and I come hard.

"Fuck...Renzo," I scream as my body clenches around him so tightly that he roars while emptying himself inside of me.

He slows but continues to thrust until I can feel both our fluids dripping from me. Pulling himself out of me, he whispers into my ear, "You look fucking beautiful with my marks on your ass and my cum running down your thighs."

Fighting back the need to grimace while bending to pick up my dress from the floor, "This doesn't change anything. I'm not yours, and I still fucking hate you."

Crossing the hall, I enter my room and shut the door. I simply shake my head at myself as I stand with my back against the door.

What the fuck are you doing, Ava?

Chapter Nineteen

LORENZO

"You tell yourself what you need to hear," I whisper to myself eyeing her beautifully marked ass as she crosses the hall to her room.

Pulling on my boxer briefs, I head into the bathroom. I grab a washcloth and dampen it with hot water before grabbing a bottle of aloe and heading across the hall.

My knuckles gently rap on the door, and I hear Ava immediately on the other side as though she made it no further than entering the room.

"I'm coming in, *piccola pesca*."

Turning the knob, I open the door to find her standing just past the door, still naked.

"What do you want?" she snaps back at me with a look on her face I cannot quite distinguish, "I'm not letting you fuck me again."

"You will fuck me again...and soon," my words confident as I step closer to her, "but that is not what I came over here for."

Tossing the aloe onto the bed, I take another step and slide my fingers along her jaw before kneeling before her. Placing one hand on her outer hip, I use the other to slide the washcloth up her thighs, cleaning myself from her.

"While I do enjoy watching my cum run down your thighs, when this happens again I will ensure I wear a condom. We wouldn't want you getting pregnant."

"I can't get pregnant. I have a Nexplanon," the words vomit from her mouth, as she physically tries to stop them. In response a small smile spreads on my face.

She continues, "It doesn't matter, because that is never happening again."

"On the bed," my words soft as I finish cleaning her thighs, "Get on your stomach. Let me tend to my marks."

Dropping her clothes to the floor, as much as she denies whatever this is, she follows my commands and walks towards the bed. I pull back the blanket, making ample room for her to lay on the sheets.

Grabbing the aloe, I squeeze some into my hand. I rub my hands together for a moment to warm the aloe before gently placing my palms on her upper thigh. She winces at my touch, the fresh marks sore.

"This will help."

Leaning down, I gently kiss the exposed skin between my palms before smoothing my hands over her thigh, delicately covering my marks with the soothing lotion. I repeat the process until I have gently rubbed lotion over all of the marks left behind from my belt. By the time I finish, her body is lax against the bed, exhausted as the adrenaline leaves her body.

After wiping my hands on the washcloth, I pull the blanket over her curves and up to her shoulders. Her eyelids are heavy as I push her hair from her face and tuck it behind her ear.

"What are you doing?" her words groggy as she is nearly drifting off to sleep.

Leaning down, I place a gentle kiss on her temple and whisper, "I take care of what's mine."

"I'm not yours," she mumbles back as her eyes close.

"You keep telling yourself that, *piccola pesca*," I whisper before grabbing my things and quietly leaving her room.

Crossing the hall back to my room, I see V down the hall.

"I was coming to check on Ava," her eyes pass over my nearly naked body, "but I'm thinking she might be feeling better."

Obviously pleased with herself, she winks as a broad smile spreads across her face.

"Did you really buy her?" she questions.

"Is this really a conversation we are going to have while I'm in my underwear in the hallway?"

"That's not a no," she responds, "maybe not now, but this is definitely a conversation we are having."

There is no use arguing with Princess V, she always gets her way. I give her a nod before entering my room and shutting the door. Grabbing my clothes from the floor, I place them in the hamper with the washcloth before putting the aloe back in the cabinet and hanging my belt in the closet.

I debate showering but, while slightly masked by the smell of aloe on my hands, I can still smell Ava on my skin. Relishing in the scent, I climb into my bed and slide between the sheets – sheets I hope to make smell like her soon.

Closing my eyes, her scent, and thoughts of claiming her body again, flood my mind. Sleep is definitely not happening any time soon.

Climbing back out of bed, I grab a pair of sweatpants from my closet before heading downstairs. Passing my father's office, I hear his voice, "What are you doing Lorenzo?"

"Just getting a drink," I respond stopping in the doorway.

"Your meetings?"

"I met with all of the families. I can't rule any of them out. It could be any of them. It could be none of them."

"With every hit," he stands from his desk, "we look weak. And you know what happens to weak families."

"Yes, Papa," I respond as he passes towards the doorway.

"I know who she is," he pats my arm, "and I don't care. I actually think she might be good for you."

Chapter Twenty

AVALIE

TWO WEEKS LATER...

The sun is blazing through the window when I begin to wake up.

Why the fuck is it so bright?

Groaning from soreness as I roll over, I turn the clock on the nightstand towards me. Ten o'clock. Swinging my feet over the bed and throwing back the covers, a chill hits my naked body.

Naked? Oh fuck!

The sudden realization of why my ass cheek is so tender hits me.

That wasn't a dream.

I let him fuck me, again.

Who am I kidding? I was dying for him to fuck me again.

I needed it. I needed it so badly that I would have begged him for it.

No matter how many times I tell myself it is never happen again, it happens again. Twice yesterday even. My brain might be thinking, "no," but my body is screaming, "fucking take me."

Even with how sensitive the skin is on my backside, my pussy clenches and throbs at the thought of the yearning look in his eyes, needing me. The gentle caress of his hands and how they ground me. The abrasive words from his mouth as he commands me. The pain of his belt on my skin as he frees my mind. The way his cock stretches me every time he presses inside of me. He takes what he needs from my body but gives me everything I did not even know mine needed in return.

For fuck's sake, Ava.

Renzo is a criminal, heir to a crime syndicate even. He takes women as payment for debts. He is not the type of man you catch feelings for...even if he is tall...so muscular...has eyes that pierce your soul...plays your body like he has been practicing his whole life...gives orgasms so strong it feels like the world is imploding...

Shit! Where was I?

Stepping into the shower, I grab the loofa and begin to scrub my skin. I rake the loofa so hard over my body, it's like I am trying to unsuccessfully scrub Renzo from my skin and thoughts.

"It's about time you got up."

"Jesus Christ," I scream as Renzo's voice in the bathroom startles me, "Do you ever fucking knock?"

"You have nothing I haven't seen before and or don't plan on seeing plenty more of in the future. You are mine, *piccola pesca*."

"For the last time," I huff, "I am not yours."

"Keep telling yourself that," he closes the shower door, "Finish up. There are clothes on the bed for you, and we have somewhere to be."

"What?" I call back at him, but he either does not hear me or he opts to ignore me.

Did he say somewhere to be?

Not even knowing if I heard him right, I quickly finish my shower. After drying my hair and throwing on a little make-up, I walk into the bedroom to find Renzo waiting patiently on my bed next to a blue floral maxi dress, strappy heeled sandals, and beautiful sapphire blue lace undergarments.

Renzo rises from the bed as I approach, "Or we could stay here."

Grabbing my towel, he pulls me against his body. Every ounce of me that keeps saying 'not again' disintegrates as I breathe him in and he wraps his fingers around my neck.

"Fight it all you want," his fingers slide down the slit in the towel until he's brushing over my hip, "You can't deny how much you like being mine."

"I. Am. Not. Yours."

"Are you sure about that?" the corner of his mouth lifts into a smirk.

"Absolutely," my voice flat.

His eyes fixated on mine; his tongue slowly licks across his lower lip. His fingers slide along my hip, grazing over my thigh, before sliding inside of me with ease.

With two fingers deep inside of me, the hand around my neck slides into the hair at the nape of my neck and grips firmly. A gasp exits my mouth as Renzo pulls my hair, painfully yanking my head back.

His tongue plunges into my mouth as his fingers curl violently inside of me bringing me to the cusp of an orgasm.

I moan into his mouth. In response, he tightens the grip in my hair and begins to firmly rub his thumb over my clit while continuing to curl his fingers inside of me.

My body is currently a war of pleasure and pain. Renzo's touch blissfully painful as he continues to play with my body.

Dragging his lips from mine, he kisses towards my ear, "Who owns this cunt?"

He vigorously pulls and thrusts his curling fingers as my walls begin to squeeze around his fingers. Relentlessly, he does not ease up. He only increases his speed.

"I asked you a question," he sharply nips at my neck, "Who does this cunt belong to?"

"You...it belongs...to you," the words quiver from my lips as pleasure wins the war raging inside of me and my orgasm consumes me.

My legs are shaking as he slowly pulls his fingers from me and drags my wetness over my tender clit. He rubs them across his lips, leaving them glistening with my wetness, before placing them against my lips.

His tongue darts from his mouth and he moans, "Say it again. Who does that sweet fucking cunt belong to?"

"You," my gaze heated as I watch him slowly lick my arousal off his lips. His wet fingers slide into my mouth, the sweet tang of my own arousal coating my tongue.

"Suck," his words so demanding that my pussy clenches as I wrap my lips around his fingers. His fingers slide along my tongue as I clean them of my arousal.

"Later," he says slowly pulling his fingers from my mouth, "I'm going to watch as you suck your cream off every inch of my cock. For now, get dressed, you have a day of playing nice ahead of you."

The smirk on his face is devious as he walks into the bathroom leaving me to dress.

Shit. Did that just actually happen?

The one thing I said would never happen. The one thing I actually meant and intended to follow through on. And still, I caved and said exactly what he wanted. I told him he owns me.

Chapter Twenty-One

LORENZO

Leaving her to get dressed, I head into my room to grab my Beretta from the safe in my closet. I have mundane errands to run today, but as the only outside she has seen in weeks is the garden, I thought it might be nice to take her out into the city for a bit. Maybe give her the opportunity to see who I am outside of the four walls of this house.

...Mine.

It might have been coerced, but she said it. She is mine. She knows that she is mine. She might still be fighting it, but she *wants* to be mine.

It might take time, but she is going to admit that she is mine when I am not buried deep inside of her.

Sliding the gun into the front of my pants, I head back into the hallway to collect Ava.

I am quite pleased when I find her standing in the hallway. The dress clinging to her chest and flowing from her hips, the slit running up her left side just barely providing me a glimpse of the silky-smooth skin of her thigh. A thigh I intend to devour later this evening.

"So," she looks at me smugly, "What kind of mafia shit are we going to do today?"

"Mafia shit?" I question back at her, "We don't call it mafia shit."

"Brooding crime shit?" She smirks as she turns and begins to walk down the hallway. My eyes fully fixated on her hips as they sway her ass back and forth with each step.

She is fucking infuriating.

She pauses when she reaches the front door, waiting for me.

Opening the door, I gesture for her to go in front of me. She pauses. It is in this moment that I realize she cannot be mine like this. This whole time she has lived in fear of what would happen to her if she steps outside of this house, even the past couple of weeks as I thought something was happening between us. She cannot really ever be mine if she thinks it's because she has to be.

Stepping through, taking the lead, I reach my hand out for hers and kindly say, "Come." Placing her hand in mine, she slowly steps across the threshold. Keeping her hand in mine, I walk her towards the garage where Massimo has already pulled my car out front for me.

Opening the door, I help lower her into the soft leather of the seat. Grabbing the seatbelt, I lean over her while dragging it across her body before clicking it in place.

"I'm capable of doing that myself," she grumbles back at me.

"Capable or not," my fingers glide under her chin, "I take care of what's mine."

"I am not yours."

Grabbing firmly on her chin, I tilt her head up towards mine, "I believe it was only a few minutes ago you told me that I own your cunt."

"My cunt, maybe," her voice trying to be firm, "but not me."

Getting into the car myself, I gun the engine and slip the car into gear before placing my right hand on her knee, slipping my fingers between the slit of her dress and sliding my hand up her thigh.

"You are mine."

You will admit it to yourself, soon enough.

Chapter Twenty-Two

AVALIE

Renzo squeezes my thigh as we take a sharp turn towards the gate. The internal struggle of pushing his hand away or allowing him to continue to grip my thigh is overwhelming.

My brain continues to tell me that everything about this is wrong. He bought me. He owns me. He is using me.

But my body is continuously yearning for more of what he does to me. The way he makes me feel.

Feel...it's not just my body.

As though he can read my thoughts, he squeezes my thigh again. His thumb slowly drags back and forth over my skin as he drives. This touch is different. It is not bruising, demanding, or even sexual. It's soft, tender, and comforting.

Intimate.

The feel of his skin on mine, just touching me, I like it. The feeling is foreign, but it makes me feel wanted.

As much as I continue to try and fight it, I know he is right. I do not know exactly when it happened, but I don't really hate him anymore. I do not want to run from him. It's been at least a week, if not longer, since thoughts of getting away from here filled my head. I didn't stop because it was hopeless, but rather that I don't want to.

I am pulled from my thoughts when the car comes to stop. Renzo has pulled to the side of the road in front of a rundown nightclub with a for sale sign out front.

Helping me from the car, he leads me to the door with his hand on the small of my back. Inside the club is a gorgeous man that looks like a slightly younger and slightly less muscular version of Renzo.

"Welcome home brother," Renzo calls across the club getting his attention.

He turns around, but his attention is solely focused on me as he eyes me up and down.

"Did you bring me a welcome home present?" He reaches towards me as Renzo pulls my back flush against him.

"Sorry Carlo," he squeezes my shoulders and places a kiss on my neck, "this one is mine."

"Too bad, *bella*," he takes my hand in his and brings it to his mouth before placing a gentle kiss above my knuckles, "You are way too beautiful for this asshole."

"I'm not his," Even I don't really believe the words coming from my mouth.

"That's enough, playboy," Renzo jokingly shoves him away from me, "Show me this place."

"I know it doesn't look like much now," Carlo walks towards the dilapidated bar, but I think this place could be amazing with a little renovation."

"This is the mafia shit?" The disappointment obvious in my tone.

Carlo laughs, "Apparently you are aware what my family does for a living."

"Carlo is looking for an investor," Renzo turns to me, "but if it's 'mafia shit' you are really looking for I have another place we can go after this."

The smile on my face is bigger than it should be. But the thrill of finding out what Renzo actually does, besides abducting women against their will and fucking them senseless, is intriguing as hell.

"I see you like the idea of a little danger," he whispers into my ear before following Carlo further into the bar.

I flop on a barstool while I wait for them to wander around the place. Various conversations about remodels, aesthetics and business ideas carry on for hours. By the time Renzo comes back to my barstool, the boredom must be readable on my face.

"You look bored," Renzo says sliding himself between my legs, "I have a fix for that."

Pushing him back from me, I stand up from the stool.

"Mafia shit," I whine, "Please, I am so bored. I thought leaving the house today would be exciting."

"Trust me," the sultry words flow from his tongue, "Me fucking you on the bar would definitely be exciting."

Playfully, I shove him away from me.

"Are you sure?" he questions me, "The work I do is, well, messy."

"Show me," I taunt him.

Pulling his phone from his pocket, he makes a call.

"Luca is on the other side of town," he tells me, "He is going to wait for us."

Renzo drags me from the bar to the car, obviously excited about where we are headed. He quickly makes his way through city traffic, taking us across Brooklyn Bridge into an area of the city that I have never been to before.

We drive through some shady streets until we come to a warehouse that looks as though it has been unoccupied for at least a few years. It is rusted and several of the windows are broken. If it weren't for the light shining through one of the windows upstairs, I would question why he brought us here.

Renzo opens my door, helps me from the car, and shuts the door. Using his body, he presses me against the car as his fingers curl around my throat.

Fuck, I love this feeling. Somewhere this went from being scary to possessively hot.

His body firmly pressing against mine, he gently squeezes his fingers while simultaneously taking the breath from my mouth. His tongue devours my mouth before leaving me needy and wanting as he pulls away from me.

"There is no coming back from this, *piccola pesca*," he steps back from me, "You are about to see all of who I am."

As much as I deny it to myself, I know that my heart is quickly falling for this man. While it is absolutely terrifying, I want – no I need – to know exactly who Renzo is. I need to know what he is capable of.

"Show me...," my voice firm in my request.

Grabbing my hand, he walks with me into the warehouse. Crossing the vast open area of the main floor, we head to the stairs running along the back of the building.

After the first two steps, he stops and turns, looking back at me. I see the hesitation in his eyes, and hope that he sees mine are brimming with a mixture of trepidation and excitement.

I squeeze his hand, urging him to go on. Taking my cue, he turns and continues up the to the landing where Luca is waiting.

Behind Luca is a man with his wrists wrapped in chains and his naked body is hanging from them. While his face looks brave, the look in his eyes is of absolute terror.

"You brought her?" Luca questions as though I am not standing right there.

"She wants to know who I am. And to fully understand, we both know she needs to see it."

"You sure about that?" Luca looks towards me.

Nodding back at him, Renzo walks me towards the back of the room. When we reach the counter, he grabs my waist and lifts me onto the countertop. Pushing my knees apart, he steps between my thighs and grips his hands around my ass before planting a wet kiss on my lips.

His eyes scan over me, and I can tell that he is thinking about something. The expression on his face changes so subtly that it is almost unnoticeable as he lifts his shirt, exposing his gun to me. Pulling it from his pants, he places it onto the counter next to me. Leaving the gun, he slowly steps back from me.

His gesture is not lost on me. He trusts me. Trusts me, at least enough to know that I will not take his own gun and turn it on him. The fact that he knew that with near certainty before I did, baffles the hell out of me.

Renzo slowly the rolls the sleeves to his shirt, exposing his forearms. Detailed tattoos swirl around the veins and flexing muscles. I bite my lower lip and press my thighs together as my body reacts to the mere sight of him.

Chapter Twenty-Three

LORENZO

I don't want to hide this side of myself from her. She deserves to know what kind of man I am. Pain. Suffering. Death. This is what I do for a living, and I fucking love my job.

The pleasure that I get from inflicting pain and killing is nearly euphoric.

She has seen bits and pieces of the man I am. But will she be able to look at me the same after she sees that side of me?

Rolling up my sleeves, I look back at her one more time before getting to work. For one of the first times in my life, I feel fear. Looking at her, I am afraid this is the last time she will look at me like this.

I walk towards the man I am here to see. He is a low-level member of the Yakuza, but certain people have overheard him talking about the hits on our family, obviously piquing our interest.

"Do you know who I am?" My voice is dark as I grab a knife from the table next to his swinging body. Opting for a large one, I flip it in my hand so that the handle is facing him.

Ramming the butt of the knife into his gut, he lets out a loud grunt, as his body spins in the chains.

"I asked you a question," my voice growing increasingly angry, "Do you know who the fuck I am?"

"Lorenzo," he violently sucks in air, "Botti...celli."

"Good," I spin the knife in my palm, turning the blade towards him.

Grabbing hold of him to stop him from spinning, I press the sharp tip of the knife against his flank. Slowly applying more pressure, the tip breaks his skin and a trickle blood runs down his thigh.

Leaving the tip just inside of his skin, I continue, "What do you know about the fires?"

"Nothing," he cries, "I don't know nothing."

Plunging the knife deep into his abdomen, I quickly pull it out and press just the tip through his flesh an inch above the hole my knife was just in.

"Don't lie to me," I slightly twist the tip of the knife widening the hole, "We've heard you talking all over the city."

"I don't-," his words cut short by two quick and meticulous plunges of my knife. Each strike painful, not lethal, as I inch closer to his chest, blood now oozing down his leg.

"I thought I was clear," dragging the tip of the knife through the flesh of his chest opening a shallow wound, "Don't fucking lie to me."

My chest is heaving as I continue to drag the knife all the way to his navel, leaving a trail of blood in its wake as he screams for mercy.

"There is no mercy here," I slowly press the blade into his stomach to the hilt before twisting it. He screams in agony as the blade twists and cuts through more of his flesh.

Slowly pulling the blade from him, I momentarily turn to check on Ava to ensure this is not too much for her. Her body is bent forward, her forearms resting on her knees. My eyes scale up her body to her chest, her breathing visibly heavy. Her mouth is slightly agape, and her eyes are wide. When her gaze meets mine, all I can see is her fire and need. Her eyes are fixated on me, focused on my every move with unwavering amazement.

Fuck! Watching me work actually turns her on. That look in her eyes is undeniable.

My cock twitches as I shove the knife into his thigh, his screams immediately filling the room.

"Gregorian," he cries out with my blade still in his thigh.

"What about Gregorian?"

"Gregorian and the oyabun," he pants out through his pain, "That's all I know."

Pulling the knife from his thigh, I thrust it under his chin. Blood pools down his neck as his as the light of life slowly drains from his eyes.

"Fucking Armenians," Luca groans. And had it not been for his words, I almost would have forgotten that he was present. As the life pumped from the man hanging from the ceiling, my eyes were fixed on Ava.

Pulling the knife from him, I slide each side of the blade over the thigh of my pants as my gaze returns to Ava.

"Leave us," I command towards Luca.

"Renzo?" his voice questioning.

"Out!" I bellow back in response as I stalk towards Ava, knife still in hand. My cock has grown painfully tight against the confines of my pants.

I turn back just long enough to ensure that Luca went downstairs, before giving my full attention back to Ava.

Short heavy breaths have her breasts heaving. Most men would assume it is because she is scared or panicking over what she was watching, but the faint aroma of her arousal tells me otherwise. Her knees part as I reach her, eagerly making room for me between her thighs. I watch as her chest heaves when I step between them.

"You like watching me work?" My blood-tinged thumb slowly swipes across her lower lip, "I can smell your sweet cunt from across the room. And I can see the bloodlust in your eyes."

Ava simply stares back at me, her chest heaving increasingly faster with each breath as I slide her dress up to her thighs.

"Off," I command, and she lifts each of her thighs providing me the access I need to pull the dress from under her hips and over her head.

Chapter Twenty-Four

AVALIE

Watching Renzo torture this man should disgust me. It should scare me and be utterly repulsive. Yet he is so masterful at his craft that I cannot help but be enamored with him. He is fucking fearless. Ruthless... and his face when he looks at me.

Fuck. What is wrong with me?

By the time he kills the unknown man, my panties are soaked, my pussy is throbbing, and I can barely breathe.

He demands Luca leave us as he wipes the bloody blade across the thigh of his pants and stalks towards me. My heart is pounding in my chest as he gets closer to me. With each step, the splatter of blood across his body becomes more apparent. Regardless of his appearance, my knees part for him when he reaches me.

He swipes the metallic taste of blood across my lower lip, before pulling my dress over my head and tossing it to the floor.

Renzo places the tip of the knife against my chin and slowly rakes it down my neck, scratching my skin as it drags. My breaths are ragged as the knife trails from my chest to my navel, now knowing firsthand what he is capable of doing with it. Yet my body involuntarily arches towards him, longing for his touch.

Pulling the knife away from my body, he dips a finger under the top of my panties and pulls them firmly into his palm as the knife slices through the thin straps on each of my hips, shredding them from my body. Renzo throws them to the floor as he presses my thighs wider.

Quickly undoing his belt, he unfastens his pants freeing his massive, hard cock. With his golden eyes fully fixated on mine, he drags the cool flat edge of the blade over my slit while pressing the head of his cock against my entrance. My hips rock, trying desperately to pull him inside of me, and his large hand firmly grips my hip to hold me in place.

"Careful, *piccola pesca,*" he warns as he drags the knife up towards my throat, "you need to stay still."

The head of his cock presses inside of me as the blade of the knife presses into the thin flesh under my chin. He continues to press himself into me ever so slowly until he is finally buried to the hilt. Renzo slides himself in and out of me at a slow pace. A deliberate, painfully slow pace.

"Renzo...Please," I beg as my body trembles, needing more than what he is giving me.

Ignoring my pleas, he continues his slow, steady thrusts with a devilish smirk on his face. The knife to my throat and the savage hold on my hip keeping me from moving.

My chin trembles as I watch all of him ever so slowly disappear inside of me over and over again.

"Fuck!" I cry out and my head tips back, as the tip of the knife drags between my breasts. Not cutting, but deep enough that it is leaving a dark red trail straight to where Renzo is slowly pressing inside of me again.

Tossing the knife to the ground, Renzo slaps his hand against my ass and grips it tightly as he thrusts into me hard and fast. Suddenly brutal, as he repeatedly pulls my hips hard into each fast, savage thrust.

"Oh my God!" I pant as I feel the orgasm building at my center.

"Not God," Renzo growls into my ear, "only *I* can show you to the pleasures of Heaven and the pains of Hell."

The ferocious thrusts of his cock and the grip he his has on my body are blissfully painful.

"Tell me, *piccola pesca*, do you prefer Heaven?" he groans as he continues to relentlessly pound into me while his lips travel down my neck.

"Or Hell?" He sinks his teeth through the flesh of my shoulder as he buries his cock in me.

I scream out in both pleasure and pain, as my orgasm consumes every nerve in body.

"Fuck," Renzo growls as I clench around him and rake my fingers down his shoulders.

"Fucking mine," he roars, continuing to thrust as he empties himself inside of me.

Chapter Twenty-Five

LORENZO

Ava's forehead is resting on my chest, and both of us are glistening with sweat. Her breathing still rapid, she lets out a soft groan as I slowly pull myself from her.

Gently lifting her chin to look into her eyes, "Are you okay?"

She nods back, "Just sore."

Bruises are already forming on her hips from the aggressive grip I held her with. While I am always rough, this time I lost control. There was something about her seeing me – really seeing who I am – and wanting me because of it. It did me in. I had to have her.

Bending down, I grab her dress from the floor and help her pull it back over her head. Placing her hands on my shoulders, I wrap one arm under her knees and the other around back, pulling her into my arms.

"Just because I didn't argue that I'm yours this time," she huffs at me, "doesn't mean you get to carry me everywhere. I can walk."

Ignoring her request to be put down, I kiss her forehead and carry her down the stairs.

"You need to tell me when I hurt you."

"You always hurt me," she says sarcastically while rolling her eyes, before continuing in a more sincere tone, "You didn't do anything I didn't want, and you didn't hurt me. I'm just a little sore."

Walking out of the warehouse, Luca is leaning up against his car smoking a cigarette. His eyes are judgmental when he sees me carrying Ava. I keep her in my arms until we get to the car. Gingerly setting her feet on the ground, I open the door and help her into her seat.

"I need a few minutes with Luca," I place a gentle kiss on her forehead, "and then I will take you home to take care of you."

"I'm fine," she begins to protest.

"You are mine," I silence her, "and I take care of what is mine."

Closing her door, I head towards Luca to discuss some business. He eyes me as I walk towards him, taking a long drag on his cigarette.

"What?" he exhales, "After that, I needed a fucking smoke. Shit, people down the street probably need one too."

He flicks the butt when I reach him, "That's her, right? Frank's kid?"

Luca continues when I nod my head, "I'm going to need you to explain what kind of mind-fuckery, Casanova shit you're doing. You basically bought her. And now she's suddenly coming on jobs with you and fucking you next to dead guys?"

"I'm fucking charming."

"It probably doesn't hurt that you have a shit ton of money and a huge cock," he laughs.

"Funny," I pause, getting back to business, "Gregorian?"

"I've been out here trying to figure that out," Luca rubs his jaw, "I cannot come up with a single reason why Gregorian would be spending time with the head of the Yakuza. Their families hate each other."

"That was my thought as well. I say we stir up some shit and see what happens."

"I like the sound of this."

"Make sure he makes his way back home, with a little note from Gregorian. We'll see what happens from there. Call me when it's done."

Luca heads back into the warehouse with a strange smirk on his face.

This should be interesting.

Chapter Twenty-Six

AVALIE

Renzo is different.

This is a side of him that I have never seen. Yes, he always tends to me to ensure that I am okay after we... um...play? But never like this.

My feet have not touched the ground since the warehouse. Renzo carried me into the house and up to his room. And even now my feet are not on the floor.

Renzo is sitting on the edge of the bathtub with me in his lap, while he draws a bath. His hand delicately slides from my thigh, down my calf to my ankle before unstrapping my heel. Throwing it to the floor, he gently rubs my foot. He proceeds to do the same with the other, before gingerly rubbing his hand back up my leg to my thigh bringing the dress with it. With ease, he removes it from my body, leaving me naked on his lap.

With his lips on my neck, his finger traces over the scratches left behind from his knife, *"Bellisima.* So beautiful."

Turning his body, he gently lowers me into the tub before standing. I watch as he slowly unbuttons his shirt. Slowly revealing his pronounced pecs and then each ripple of his hard abs. Throwing the shirt to the floor, he kicks off his shoes as he unbuckles his belt. Undoing his button and zipper, he pushes his pants to the floor. Standing in just his black boxer briefs is a perfect specimen of man. He is built like a fucking statue.

Well, like a statue but significantly more well-endowed.

"Renzo?" my eyes questionably drop to the bulge in his boxers.

"I'm not getting in Ava," he reassures me as he puts his feet in the tub, "Now move forward a little."

Scooching forward, I deadpan, "I was just going to ask what you feed that thing."

Grabbing below my chin, he chuckles as he pulls me back between his thighs. Gently tilting my head back until I am looking in his eyes, he bends down and kisses my lips.

"This beautiful, fucking sassy mouth. Your sweet fucking cunt," he pauses while he pours water over my hair.

"And someday soon," he gently lathers shampoo in my hair, "that perky round ass of yours."

We are silent as he rinses my hair and repeats the process with conditioner, before delicately washing every inch of my skin.

He steps from the tub, his wet legs pooling water on the floor, "Soak for a moment. I'm going to take a quick shower to wash off."

It is only at this moment, I realize that he still has blood splattered across his face and neck. While washing me, he was also cleaning off the blood he had left on my skin.

What the hell is wrong with you Ava? How are you okay with all of this?

Before I have much more time to think and actually deal with everything running through my head, Renzo is standing at the side of the tub with a towel wrapped around his waist, his skin glistening from his shower. Holding out a hand, he helps me from the tub, dries me off and wraps me in a towel.

Lifting me at the waist, he carries me over to the sink and sets me on the counter. Pulling a wide-toothed comb from the drawer he carefully detangles my hair.

Placing the comb back, he opens another drawer and removes a bottle of lotion.

"Renzo..."

"Shhhh, *piccola pesca.* Just let me take care of you."

Renzo soothingly spreads the lotion over every inch of my skin. His touch is gentle and caring – not sexual. When he finishes, he returns the lotion to the drawer and lifts me into his arms.

Carrying me from the bathroom, I expect him to return me to my room. Instead, he carries me to his bed. Placing me on the ground, he pulls back the covers before removing both of our towels. Climbing into the bed, he pulls me in with him.

His arms wrap around my body as he pulls my back flush against him. I feel his fingers tuck my hair behind my ear and pull it away from my neck, immediately replacing it with his warm breath as he nuzzles against me. His fingers lingering over my body as he holds me against him.

Unable to stop, his name questionably falls from my mouth, "Renzo?"

Pulling me tighter against him, "I've told you; I take care what is mine. You, *piccola pesca*, you are mine."

"It's just," I pause not knowing how to continue, "You've never been like this with me. This is...not like you."

"It is," he whispers against my face, "This is who I am for you, and only you."

Renzo rolls my body so that we are face to face before pulling me against him again. His fingers pushing the hair from my face as he continues, "You needed to be ready to see who I am. I torture. I kill. And I enjoy it. I became a dark and evil man, because that is the man my family needed me to be. That is who I am...for them. What little good is left inside of me, that is who I saved for you. The man that you need me to be for you. That is the type of man I want to be for you."

He places a gentle kiss on my forehead and pulls me into his chest as our legs intertwine.

"Does that mean no more leather and chains?" My own giggle interrupting my attempt at a serious tone.

"Not a chance," he pulls me closer, "I need something to keep your bratty mouth in line."

"Good," I mumble back into his chest.

"Then go to sleep."

"One more question," I proceed to ask groggily, "What is *piccola pesca*?"

"What do you think it is?"

"To be honest, I really thought it meant pain in the ass," he briefly chuckles at my answer, "but that doesn't seem right anymore."

"It's Italian for little peach," his hands roam on my back, "You are my little peach. Sometimes you are sweet. Sometimes you are sour."

I am about to respond when his hands firmly grip my ass and pull my hips into him, "and the first time I met you, I could not take my eyes off this perfectly round ass. So, I suggest you go to sleep before I fuck your pretty little peach of an ass to sleep."

Chapter Twenty-Seven

LORENZO

Ava stirs from her sleep as I slowly pull the sheets towards the end of the bed. Revealing her beautiful body to me inch by beautiful fucking inch. She attempts to sit up, but quickly realizes that her wrists and ankles are shackled to the bed.

"What the fuck, Renzo?" she growls at me causing the corner of my mouth to tick up.

"Such a foul mouth," my fingers trail up her body, "Do I need to gag you to teach you to watch your mouth?"

Light sparkles in her eyes at the thought of being both bound and gagged.

Fucking hell. It isn't really even punishment with her.

Suddenly, a loud commotion from downstairs draws my attention from Ava.

"Renzo!," I hear Luca calling for me.

"Don't you dare leave me like this," Ava spits out at me.

"Mmmm...you thinking all day about what I plan to do to you when I return," I walk towards the door, "And me knowing you are just here waiting."

"Renzo!"

Cracking the door, I yell, "Be down in two minutes."

Returning to the bed, I quickly undo the shackles restraining Ava, "Just know, I plan to put you back here very soon."

"I look forward to it," she kisses my cheek before sliding off the bed and wrapping the sheet around her body.

Quickly pulling on a pair of jeans and a Henley, I pull Ava close and kiss her.

"Get dressed," I pull open the door, "And come downstairs."

Turning the hallway towards the stairs, I quickly realize that the majority of the family is in the foyer.

"What the fuck is going on?" I call over to Luca.

"Six more places got hit last night," he informs me, "One of them was Carmine's."

"Fuck. Casualties?"

"Six guys so far," Luca replies, "and two guys unaccounted for."

"Names?" I question.

"I'll find out."

"Then send someone to check on their families."

"You got it."

Ava makes her way down the stairs, and I nod my head gesturing for her to come stand next to me.

"What's going on?" she questions.

"*Abbassa i toni,*" Sal calls over everyone, "Quiet down."

As if God himself has spoken, side conversations are immediately halted, and all attention is on him. The respect his power commands is unlike any other.

"This shit ends now," his voices bellows throughout the hall, "This family will not be seen as weak. If we don't know which family is behind this, fuck 'em all!"

I feel Ava's fingers slip in between mine before she squeezes my hand. Turning towards her, I immediately notice the concerned look on her face.

"Fuck 'em all," Sal repeats, "We hit them all on Monday. The Russians. The Armenians. The Triad. The Yakuza. Fucking all of them. Take the weekend, get your families situated. Monday night, we go to war."

Ava's hand squeezes mine again.

"This isn't the first time," I whisper to her, "and it will not be the last. You are safe here."

"Are you sure?"

"This house is a fortress. A well protected fortress. No one is getting in here."

Tucking a strand of hair behind her ear, I answer the next question I know she is hesitant to ask, "You don't need to worry about me either. You won't be getting rid of me that easily."

Nearly everyone has left as my father commanded, heading home to spend the day with their families in case it is their last. All that remains with us are my father, Luca, V, Carlo, and Dante.

"Because I don't quite trust you to follow my instructions," my father turns to V, "Dante will be increasing his presence. He will be watching over you day and night until these things are situated."

"You've got to be kidding me," V huffs back at him.

"I don't kid about the safety of my family. He will be taking you out of town to some place safe this afternoon."

"Seriously," V scoffs, "I have shit to do this week."

"Venecia," Sal's voice loud and firm, "This is not up for debate. I suggest you go pack a bag."

"Fucking bullshit," V mumbles as she stomps up the stairs.

"Dante is more than capable of taking Avalie as well," Sal turns towards us.

"No Papa," I squeeze Ava's hand, "She's staying here with me. I trust her not to leave this house without me."

"Unfortunately, I can't say the same of your sister."

"Giancarlo," he turns towards my brother, "I am putting a guy on you as well. He'll be posing as your driver as to not raise any suspicion."

Carlo nods. Unlike V, he knows that arguing this new arrangement is absolutely futile. "Thank you for the discretion."

Chapter Twenty-Eight

LORENZO

Most of the weekend was a blur, the days spent planning a well-calculated strike against all of the other families and determining how to hit them all.

"Don't wait up, *piccola pesca*," I pull Ava against me, "It is going to be late by the time we get back."

"Wake me when you get back?"

"Before or after I tie you back up?"

A coy smile breaks on her face as I lean down to kiss her.

"Lets go," Luca calls to me, "it's almost midnight."

Stepping outside of the house, I see that the last man is getting into a car to head out.

Each of the cars pull through the gates of the estate and begin to scatter throughout the city, slowly making their way onto the turf of the Triad, Yakuza, Armenians, and Russians.

Three or four primary, and well-known, fronts for each family are getting hit tonight. At two, we burn them all. One coordinated strike, hitting them all simultaneously, leaving no one the opportunity to defend themselves or retaliate.

Luca and I are currently heading towards a bike garage that is a well-known front and hangout for many of the Yakuza members. Luca flips off the headlights as he pulls up to the curb down the street. From here, we have a good, yet discreet, view of the garage.

"It's dark," Luca says, "most nights this place a party."

"I know," my brows furrow as I respond.

My Sig is resting on my thigh, my finger flipping the safety on and off as I watch at the vast nothingness through the window. Nearly thirty minutes passes, and we don't see a single person or any sign movement inside.

"Something isn't right," I mumble to Luca as I quietly climb from the car.

He is immediately climbing from the driver's seat and is standing next to me on the sidewalk.

"Fuck it," he says as he starts walking towards the building. I immediately walk with him.

The complete lack of streetlights or outdoor lighting make concealing our approach easy. We both peer through a window on the side of the building, and it is pitch black inside the garage – not a person in sight.

"Alright," I walk towards the back door and shoot the lock, "Fuck it."

If anyone is here, they now know we are too. Luca uses his body to push through the door, and I am immediately on his heels. We are the only sounds echoing through this building. With my back against the wall, I flip the light switch. The halogen lights crackle and flicker as they begin to turn on, quickly showing us that this place truly is currently vacant.

"What the fuck?" Luca grumbles.

Pulling my phone from my pocket, I text Papa.

> Something isn't right. This place is empty.

"Empty or not," I start grabbing anything flammable and tossing it to the floor, "fucking torch it."

As if I just unleashed a kid in a candy store, Luca is immediately grabbing for gas cans and tossing their contents along the walls. Luca leads a trail of gasoline towards the backdoor as I finish tossing papers to the floor.

Luca pulls a carton of cigarettes from his pocket and taps it on his hand before pulling one out and placing it to his lips. He tips the carton towards me, and I decline as he lights the one in his mouth. After taking a couple of long, hard drags he flicks it into the pool of gasoline by the door.

The cigarette ignites a blue flame, which immediately follows the gas trail through the warehouse. Within minutes, the flames are dancing along the walls. By the time we make our way back to the car, the entire building is engulfed in flames.

Pulling the phone back from my pocket, there is no response from Papa.

It is done

I text him as we begin our drive back to the estate.

Chapter Twenty-Nine

AVALIE

A loud bang startles me from my sleep. Rolling over, the clock on the nightstand reads two a.m.

Bang. Bang.

What the fuck was that?

It sounds like fireworks are going off in the yard. Sliding from the bed, I pull on my robe and head towards the window in an attempt to see what is going on. The glass is cool as I lean against it, seeing nothing but darkness.

I jump back from the window as two motorcycles ride from the tree line towards the house. Flashes of light come from them as I hear the sound of more fireworks.

Gunshots, Ava. Those are gunshots.

Running from the window, I cross the hall into Renzo's room. Heading straight to his closet, I go to the dresser he showed me earlier today. He had assured me I would never need them because I was safe here, but still he showed me where he kept several more handguns. Pulling open the drawer, I grab for a pistol.

The next of gun shots is louder, so much louder.

They are in the house.

Quietly closing the closet door, I walk to the back of the closet. Bracing my back against the wall, I aim the gun towards the door. My hands tremble as I prepare to protect myself from whoever might be on the other side.

The chaos on the other side of the door is progressively getting louder. Closer. My heartbeat is thumping in my ears so loud it is almost drowning out all of the other noises echoing through this house.

My breathing stops as I watch the knob turn on the closet door. The door opens revealing a thin man, dressed in leather, wearing a motorcycle helmet. My hands are shaking as I fire off a shot, missing him completely. Firing again, it grazes his helmet, but does not faze him. Lowering the gun slightly, I fire it again. This one strikes him in the shoulder, twisting his body, but he keeps coming. I fire again and again, before his body drops to the floor at my feet. Blood is quickly pooling around him.

Run, Ava!

My brain is screaming at me to run, but my feet feel as though they are encased in concrete. After what feels like an eternity, I step over the body on the floor. My stomach turns, when I feel my bare footstep into the warm sticky puddle of blood.

Beginning to run, my wet foot slides on the wood floor almost causing me to fall. Regaining my balance, I sprint down the hallway before taking the stairs two at a time. Slipping into the library, I make my way to the garden. The grass is cool and wet under my feet, making it difficult to run.

I have no idea where I am going, but I just run. My only plan for right now is to get away from the men that have swarmed this house. I hear a commotion behind me, and without looking I know they have spotted me. I keep running towards the trees, my robe blowing behind me in the wind.

Any thoughts I have of outrunning these men quickly leaves me when I hear motorcycles rapidly closing the distance behind me. Turning as I run, I fire towards them, almost certain I will not make contact with any of them.

Pulling the trigger again, nothing happens. The gun is empty. It drops from my hand as I continue running, hoping desperately to make it to the trees.

Two motorcycles pull in front me and two stay behind, quickly boxing me in, my sprint coming to a stop. I stand in the center of the four of them, completely out of breath – both from running and because I am absolutely scared out of my mind in this moment.

Nearly in sync, they all step from their bikes and close the distance between us. Immediately surrounded by the four of them, I scream even though I know there isn't anyone left here to save me.

I push at them and try to fight out of their hold.

"This doesn't have to difficult," I hear one of them say through their helmet.

"Well, it sure as shit isn't going to be easy," I spit back as I knee him in the groin. It doesn't take him down, but I clearly hear him grunt.

Feeling smug and a little proud of myself, I swing at one of the other men. I turn back around just in time to realize that the guy I kneed is about to headbutt me with his helmet.

Fuck.

I try to fight it, but the pain is buzzing through my skull. Dizziness buckles my knees, as my vision quickly fades to black.

Chapter Thirty

LORENZO

Luca and I are a few minutes into our drive back to the estate, but I just cannot shake this feeling.

"Something isn't right," I say to Luca as pull my phone from my pocket, trying once again to call Sal.

This time he answers, "Everything good?"

"Job is done, but no one was home," I respond keeping things vague. It's a burner phone, but you can never be too safe.

"No one?" he questions.

"No. Completely vacant. Were they at the other house?"

"No. The whole family must be out of town. We'll be back in forty, you?"

"Something feels off," I look at the street signs before I respond to his question, "About thirty minutes."

"We'll talk then."

Before I can say anything further, Luca steps on the accelerator. He knows what I am thinking, even if it is crazy.

No one is stupid enough to try to hit our home.

Pulling up to the estate, the iron gates are open and there are no guards. Luca guns the engine and speeds towards the house.

It's a fucking bloodbath. Several guards are laying on the stone steps leading into the house, and the front door is wide open.

Luca has barely come to a stop when I jump from the car. "Ava," I yell as I run through the foyer, stepping over several more bodies. I run to her room first, swinging open the door and finding it completely empty, the bed having been slept in. Turning to my room, the door is open and things have been tossed around.

"Avalie!" I call out again as I enter the room. After checking the room and bath, I head to the closet and am surprised to find a body on the floor. He's a smaller man wearing a motorcycle helmet.

Fucking Yakuza. Good for you, piccola pesca!

Stepping closer to the body, I notice the small bloody footprints heading out of the room. Turning, I quickly follow them back to the stairs and to the library. The door heading out to the garden is wide open.

Smart, Ava.

Heading into the garden, I am filled with fucking rage when I see the tire tracks running from the garden and through the yard.

They fucking ran her down like a dog.

"Fuck!" I scream into the night.

Sal and Luca are entering the garden as I approach the house.

"Avalie?" Sal questions.

"Call the oyabun," I push past Sal and walk into the house, "Tell him if she isn't back here, unharmed, within in an hour, they all fucking die. Every last one of them."

I don't even question if my father will do as I asked – or commanded. He will call the head of the Yakuza and demand they return Avalie to us.

This is how he lost my mother. This was why he almost burned this whole fucking city to the ground. He knows I will turn the streets red with rivers of blood before I scorch this whole fucking city to find her. He knows that she is mine and there is nothing I will not do to ensure she gets back to me.

"And Luca, start checking security footage. See if you can find anything."

I am about to start searching bodies when my phone rings, *unknown number.*

"Lorenzo," I answer.

"Renzo," I immediately place the voice as Dmitriy, "I heard about your house."

Chapter Thirty-One

AVALIE

I rub my hands along my forehead as I groggily wake up. My head is throbbing and my temple, which took the brunt of the helmet, is tender to the touch.

"I'm sorry about that," a feminine voice says from the other side of the room, "I had been very clear that they were not to hurt you."

Startled to find that I am not alone, I sit up, surprised to find that I am not restrained in any way. I am on a soft leather couch and have a blanket covering over my legs.

Is everyone this courteous when they abduct someone? I mean, this is twice now and it's really not that bad.

Jesus, Ava!

Looking around, my surroundings are not familiar. There is a single light by the couch illuminating part of the room. The office is ornate – leather, mahogany, marble – wherever I am it belongs to someone with money. Lots of money.

"It's good to see you, Avalie," the woman from across the room speaks again.

It takes a moment for my pounding head to register what she is saying.

"Do I know you?" I question to the unknown woman in the dark, my own voice cutting through my head. I strain my eyes, but I am unable to clearly see the woman sitting opposite me in the dark.

"Yes," she flatly replies, "You have not seen me in quite some time, but I have been keeping an eye on you."

Struggling to try to place her voice, I hear the leather crinkle under her as she stands. Her heels click across the marble floor as she begins to close the distance between us. Even as she approaches, she is shrouded in the darkness.

Her feet stop at the edge of the darkness in the room, leaving me unable to see her face.

"Who are you?"

"In due time," her voice is hard, "Did they hurt you?"

"Um, yeah lady. That asshole fucking headbutted me with a helmet."

"No. Not that asshole," she lets out a quiet laugh, "The Botticelli family?"

Maybe it's the throbbing in my skull, but I am struggling to follow this conversation.

"I know how Frank had treated you," her confession surprising me, "and that was the first thing I took care of."

"Took care of?" I question, pretty sure I can piece together what she means.

"We had an arrangement," her voice is flat, "and he didn't uphold his end. He was supposed to take care of you, keep you safe from my family. Protect you. His disobedience was not acceptable."

"Him hurting you," she continues to speak as I try to put the pieces of this puzzle together, "that signed his death certificate. Learning that he had sold you to the Botticellis to pay off his own debts, that ensured his death would be slow and painful."

"Frank is dead?" I question, conflicted as to whether or not I am saddened by the loss, or happy the man who cared so little about me he could sell me is gone.

"Not yet," her voice is cold, "his pain and suffering is going to be long and drawn out before I finally end his pathetic life."

Of all things to register, my brain picks up on the fact that this woman hiding in the dark is either a ruthless killer or in charge of a bunch of ruthless killers.

"What are you going to do me?"

"Avalie," her cold voice slightly warmer, "I would never hurt you. The men that came to the Botticelli house were there to save you. They work for your father, and they were supposed to bring you safely to me."

"My father?" The words clearly a question, as I grew up my entire life under the assumption my own mother had no idea who my father was.

Her heels click on the marble floor as she slowly paces in the darkness, keeping her identity concealed from me.

"It was only a matter of time," she continues ignoring my question, "before the Botticellis found out who you really were. We had to get you out of there before that could happen. Salvatore and Lorenzo would have either killed you or used you as leverage against us."

"Renzo," I shake my head, "he would never."

"Renzo," she repeats back to me in a condescending tone, "That boy is a ruthless killer. He would not hesitate."

"Aren't you a ruthless killer?" I sarcastically reply to her.

"Yes," she replies as she slowly steps into the light.

"Yes," she replies as she slowly steps into the light.

Chapter Thirty-Two

LORENZO

"I heard about the hit on your house," Dmitriy speaks through the phone, "and I want you to know it wasn't us."

"What the fuck do you know?"

"The Andreyevs had nothing to do with this," his voice firm, "Do you understand? Nothing."

"Tell me."

"I am sharing this with you despite the fact your family attacked mine today. We are not involved in this. We don't want to go to war with you."

"Just tell me what the fuck you know, Dmitriy."

"I don't know why," he pauses to clear his throat, "but the Armenians and the Yakuza are working together."

"No. That doesn't make sense," I speak aloud more to myself than to Dmitriy, "Those two families have hated each other for decades. What could possibly unite them?"

"I don't know Renzo," Dmitriy answers my rhetorical question, "it's something big."

"Truce?" I question, "We will make amends for tonight's attack."

"I am the only one who knows it was your family," Dmitriy replies, his accent as thick as ever, "because we are old friends, I will take it as a favor owed."

"Yes. A favor owed from our family to yours," I respond, "Do you know anything about Avalie?"

"Avalie?" he questions back, "Your woman?"

"Yes," my voice firm, "They took her and I want her back."

"I will you know if I hear anything," Dmitriy's tone changes, "And we expect to be left out of the war that is about to take over this city."

"Stay out of my way, and I will ensure you are left alone," I respond before ending the call.

Heading back downstairs, I hear Sal slamming down the phone in his office. He shakes his head at me when I enter the room.

"The oyabun isn't taking my calls," Sal says still shaking his head.

"I just got off the phone with Dmitriy Andreyev," I say as I take a seat opposite his desk, "I don't know specifics, but the word on the street is that the Armenians are working with the Yakuza."

"Those families fucking hate each other, Lorenzo," he rebuts back.

"I know," I shake my head trying to figure it out.

"That guy from the warehouse," Luca interrupts, "the only thing he had to say was that Gregorian had been meeting with the oyabun."

"It just doesn't make sense," Sal replies, "What could mend decades of distain between those two families?"

Chapter Thirty-Three

AVALIE

Her face slowly becomes visible as she steps into the light, and it is almost like looking into a mirror. We have the same blond hair and blue eyes, the same slightly upturned nose, and pouty lips. Her face is older, but it's her.

I can't be...

"Mom?" My words sounding unsure as they cross over my lips.

"Hello, daughter," she responds.

"After all this time," my words stuttered as I struggle to process this information, "I had just assumed you were dead."

"Not dead dear," she sits across me on the couch.

"Then where were you?"

"Something happened with my family, and I had to go away to be safe."

"Without me?"

"Yes. My family did not know about you, and it was not going to be safe for me to be on the run with a child."

"Back up," I sputter, "You went on the run, because of your family, because it wasn't safe for me...and you chose to leave me with Frank...even though you do actually know who my father is."

Standing up from the couch, I gesture at the room we are in, "And you know people living like this, and I suffered and starved for years with Frank?"

She stands from the couch and attempts to approach me but stops when I recoil. "It wasn't safe for you then. For anyone to know who you belonged to. But things are different now."

"What do you mean, who I belonged to?"

"My real name is Karyan Gregorian," she pauses, "Your grandfather is Levon Gregorian, the head of the Armenian mob."

I step back from her until my back is against the wall, and I have no where else to go.

"Your father is Kaito Tanaka," she steps back from me and sits on the couch again, "the new oyabun of the Yakuza."

While I still do not know much about the families of this city, I have picked up a few things in the months that I have spent in the Botticelli house. There are five families or mobs in this city – the Russians, Armenians, Triad, Yakuza, and Botticellis. None of the families truly like each other. Most of them would more than happily kill the others – especially the Armenians and the Yakuza.

"You are telling me, that I am not the daughter of just one family," I pause, "but of two?"

"Yes," she crosses her legs and sits back on the couch, her heel tapping on the marble floor. "Our relationship was forbidden. When you were born, I was elated that you looked nothing like him. Because it meant that it would be easier for me to hide who you really were. I ran away from my family, from this life. I never told anyone who you were or who your father was. Had anyone known that you were a future walking treaty between the two families, there would have been a contract on you within days. I did what I did to protect you."

"To protect me?" I spit back, "You fucking left me with Frank."

"Watch your mouth," her voice quickly angers, "I am making amends for that and he will be dead by the end of the week."

"I just want to go home."

"Home?" she questions, "Back to Frank's shitty apartment?"

"No," I shake my head, "to Renzo."

"I know this is a lot to process, and I will leave you to do that. But you can never return to the Botticellis. You are a Gregorian and a Tanaka. It is not safe for you there."

Karyan stands from the couch and her heels click all the way to the door.

"I will be back in a few hours to check on you," she steps into the hall and shuts the door.

A moment later, I hear a click outside the door. Grabbing the knob, I turn it and pull the door, only to find that she did indeed just lock me inside

LORENZO

They do not know what they did taking her from me. There is literally nothing I will not do to bring her back to this house. She is mine, and I will kill everyone who tries to keep her from me.

In my room, I change into dark jeans and a black Henley. After pulling on my boots, I begin to grab my arsenal from my closet – two knives, a pistol and four extra clips.

I do not know which of the two families has her or where they are keeping her, but I will be leaving a bloody trail in my wake as I try to find her.

"Where are you going?" Sal calls to me as I pass the door to his office.

"To get Avalie," I briefly pause in his doorway.

"Wait," he stands from his desk.

"Nothing you can say will change my mind. I am going to get her."

"I'm not asking you to stay. Give me five minutes. I'm trying to reach Dante to check in on Venecia. Giancarlo and I will meet you at the car."

Not certain if they are coming to help or to try to keep me in line, I head to the garage and pull out a blacked out Suburban. Tapping my fingers on the steering wheel, I anxiously wait for them to hurry up and join me.

Within minutes, they are both walking out of the front door and toward the SUV. As they climb in, I turn to both of them, "Are you sure you want to come for this?"

"Lorenzo," Sal's eyes held firm with mine, "I built this family. I am not afraid to get a little dirty. And I have been in your shoes, I know exactly what you are about to go and do."

"We're about to get a lot dirty," I reply back to him, and he nods in acknowledgement.

From the backseat, Carlo reaches his hand out to my shoulder, "You are my brother. This might not be the side of the family business that I normally work with, but there are no limits to what I will do for my blood. I am not afraid to get dirty."

I do not have words to respond to him. I simply nod and put the SUV into drive. We may not know where the Yakuza are currently hiding out, but I sure as hell know where to find several members of the Armenians.

Leaving the estate, I drive toward Brooklyn Bridge. Within the hour, we will be in Coney Island, the heart of where the Armenians do their business.

First stop will be the Dolma Restaurant just off the boardwalk. The basement doubles as an underground twenty-four-hour poker room. It is operated and frequented by members of the Gregorian family. They might not know anything, but eventually someone will lead us to a person that does.

The sun is starting to peek over the horizon when we reach Coney Island and drive towards Dolma. As I park behind the restaurant, Sal pulls his gun from the waistband of his pants, "We got you."

The three of us slide out of the SUV and walk towards the backdoor of the kitchen. Without hesitation, Sal shoots the lock and pulls the door open for us to enter.

We stride towards the stairwell leading down to the poker room and are met with a large man who likely heard us enter the building. Lifting my gun, I shoot once before he has a chance to react to our presence. My bullet strikes the center of his forehead, and his body immediately falls to the ground.

Picking up our pace, the three of us quickly traverse the stairs before barreling into the poker room with our guns drawn. Entering first, Carlo quickly puts two bullets into the chest of one of the dealers, after which no one else makes a move for their weapon.

"I'm looking for someone," I shout as Sal and Carlo make their way around the room relieving everyone of their weapons, "And one of you assholes is going to help me find her."

Eyes follow me as I stalk around the room. Tucking the gun into the waistband of my pants, I reach for my knife and slide it between the ribs of a man whose back is facing me. The blade punctures his lung and not a sound comes from his mouth as blood trickles down his chin and he gasps for air.

"Her name is Avalie," I continue to stalk around the room determining which man to approach next, "And word has it you and the Yakuza took her from me."

"Fuck the Yakuza. And fuck your girl," a man spits from the other side of the room before Sal pumps three bullets into him. He obviously doesn't know what is going on and is going to be of no use to us.

I watch the facial expression of an older gentleman sitting at a table in the back corner. The look on his face is inquisitive, as though he is trying to figure out how we know what we do.

"What do you know old man?" I stare at him as I approach.

"I don't know shit," he grumbles back at me.

Grabbing the hair of the man sitting next to him, I yank his head back and slide the blade of my knife across his throat. Using my grip in his hair, I pull him from the seat to make room for myself to sit.

"I am not a man you want to fuck with," I stare at the older man while twirling my knife in my palm.

The fact that his eyes continue to stay fully fixed on mine tells me also is not a man to be fucked with.

Chapter Thirty-Five

AVALIE

This is fucking insane.

I have been locked in this room for hours, and I still cannot seem to comprehend everything my mother shared with me.

My estranged mother is an heiress to a crime family. The father I didn't know I had is the head of a different crime family. What does that make me? Heiress to two crime syndicates? And I'm fucking the man who will soon be taking over his family.

What the hell have you gotten yourself into Ava?

What does this mean for me and Renzo? I'm literally his enemy.

And why now? Why, after all this time, are both of my parents suddenly so concerned with me? Years of abuse by Frank and they did nothing, yet they needed to save me from the Botticellis? The first place in my life where I actually happy.

The distinct sound of heels clicking down the hallway stirs me from my thoughts. They stop just outside of the door, and I immediately hear the jingle of keys. The lock clicks and the door opens.

It is my mother...

Truth be told, I really don't know what to call her.

She has changed and freshened up from the last time I saw her. She is wearing a sleek black business dress, which is accentuated by her matching black and white snakeskin belt and stilettos. Her make-up is freshly applied, and her hair has been pulled into an updo.

With her current appearance, she could either walk the runway or create absolute havoc in the boardroom. Based on her cold demeanor, I'm quite certain she is nearly all business.

She is carrying a garment bag and a shoe box, both of which she gently places onto the couch next to me.

"I'm going to need you to get dressed, Avalie," she gestures towards the items she set next to me, "We have a big day ahead of us, and you, my dear, are going to be a very big part of it."

"And if I don't want to?" I smugly question.

"You don't want to test me daughter," she lifts the lid from the shoebox, "you will not like the outcome. And you will wind up doing exactly what it is that I am asking of you anyway."

Heeding her warning, I stand from the couch and reach for the garment bag. Unzipping it, I find a red dress in a similar style to the one that she is wearing. Inside the shoebox is a pair of black stilettos.

I'm never going to be able to walk in those.

Dropping my robe, I pull on the dress. My body tenses when Karyan reaches for the zipper at my back, but she merely zips the dress and hooks the clasp at the top.

"Come," she says to me as she walks towards the door.

Grabbing the stilettos from the box, I do as I am told and follow her. My bare feet pad across the cold marble floor as she authoritatively clicks her heels down the hallway. Halfway down the hall, she turns into a room, and I follow her.

"Sit," she commands as she gestures towards a chair at the vanity, "I need you to make yourself presentable."

As much as I do not want to listen or help her with whatever it is she is planning, I know it is in my best interests to do as she says. This woman is not a tender, loving mother looking to dote after me.

After placing the heels on the floor by the chair, I reach for the hairbrush and begin to detangle my hair. Once brushed, it lays straight and sleek over my left shoulder, the way that Renzo likes it. Fumbling through the brushes and powders, I apply a little blush and eyeshadow before sweeping on mascara.

"You always were a pretty girl," her hand brushes along my hair.

Trying not to react to her, I bend down to slide the heels onto my feet.

"Come," she holds her hand out to me, "It's almost time."

"Time for what," I hesitantly question.

"Your father and I are making the announcement to our families."

The announcement?

Standing in the stilettos, I find my balance before trying to keep pace with Karyan as she walks down the hallway. My inability to keep up in these heels becomes apparent when we reach the stairs. She reaches the bottom as I am still struggling to take a step at a time near the top.

The irritation is obvious on her face by the time I reach the bottom. She promptly turns and begins walking towards the door.

Fuck. More stairs and no railing.

At the bottom of the stairs is a large black SUV with completely blacked out windows. A large man opens the rear door and Karyan climbs in. Closing her door, he reaches for my hand to help me down the last few steps. I take it, only so I don't fall, and he walks me to the other side of the car before opening the door for me as well.

Climbing into the SUV, I am happy to finally not be standing on these heels, but scared as hell about where we are going and what she has me walking into.

Chapter Thirty-Six

LORENZO

"What is your name old man?" I shift in the chair and lean towards him.

"Razmik," He too shifts in his chair so that he is facing me, subtly letting me know that I do not scare him.

I nod my head at Sal, and he puts a bullet through the temple of the man sitting closest to him.

Turning my attention from the shot back to Razmik, "You do not appear to be afraid of me."

"I am an old man," he replies to me, "For the things I have done in this life, I know I am going to hell. I made peace with that a long time ago. I am not afraid to die."

As he finishes speaking, Carlo puts a bullet through the back of a younger guy's head, blowing out his face before his body slumps onto the table.

"But are you willing to have the blood of all of these men on your conscience?"

"Are you?" Razmik recants back at me.

"I'm Catholic," I smirk at him, "I recant for sins. And I have already found my salvation...my heaven is here on Earth."

Sal and Carlo each execute another man, the number of Armenians left in this room is quickly diminishing.

The knife that has been rolling in my palm is now firmly gripped by my fist. Lifting it, I quickly plunge the blade through the flesh just above Razmik's knee. He screams out in pain as I twist the blade and grind it against the bone.

His brow furrows and his eyes narrow as he grimaces in pain.

"It doesn't have to be like this," I slowly pull the blade out of the wound as Razmik's breathing becomes more rapid.

Sal executes another man, leaving just the three of us and Razmik in this basement.

My eyes fixed on his, I drive my knife through the skin above his other knee. It elicits a similar scream from the first.

"I just want Avalie," I lean into Razmik and press down on the handle of the blade, "I want to know where she is. And I want to know why the Armenians and Yakuza are working together to take her."

Sliding the knife from his thigh, I lift my hand and quickly shove it just above the previous wound. Sweat is beading at his hairline, as he grits his teeth and breathes through the pain.

"Razmik," I grab his chin in my hand, "You should know that I am really fucking good at my job. This can continue for hours, as my knife continues to carve through your flesh around anything that would prove to be fatal."

Withdrawing the blade yet again, I release my grip on his chin and lift my arm preparing to force the blade through his skin again.

"Wait," he pleads.

Lowering my arm, I rest it on my thigh and begin to palm the handle of the knife again.

"Talk," I demand.

Sweat drips down his forehead as he begins to sputter between his heavy breathing, "She is the key. She is the reason for the truce. She is going to bring the two families together, making them the most powerful in the city."

"She's a poor girl from the Bronx," I shake my head at him, "How in the world could she be the thing to bring these two families together?"

"She…**is**…the two families."

"What the fuck are you talking about?" I shove the blade of the knife firmly against his throat, as Sal and Carlo quickly close their distance to me.

"Avalie is Gregorian…and Tanaka," Razmik struggles to push out the words.

"Bullshit," Sal refutes his claim.

"I've carried this secret for twenty-three years. I assure you; it is not bullshit."

Sitting back, I pull my blade from his neck as he begins to spew the secret that he has been hiding from his own family.

"I'm not afraid of you killing me," Razmik states, "Because I have been waiting for my own family to come for me since they found out about her. It was only going to be a matter of time before they found out how her mother disappeared."

Chapter Thirty-Seven

AVALIE

The car ride is absolutely silent, with the exception of the tires rolling across the pavement. Karyan's focus rotates between her buzzing cell phone and gazing out the car window at the city.

I know I was just a child when she left, but woman sitting in the back of this car with me is nothing like the mother I remember. She looks like her, but that is all.

My mom was warm and caring. She never threatened me. She was the woman that would place herself between me and danger, constantly taking the punishments Frank wanted to dole out on me. I remember a woman who packed my lunches and held my hand as she walked me to school every day.

I remember love. Not just small glimpses of it, but all of it. Thinking of my mother makes me feel warm and wanted. Looking at this woman, I feel nothing but her eerie coldness and distain. There is no way that this woman ever cared for me a day in her life.

Nothing makes sense. She hasn't seen me in over a decade, yet she is colder to me than a stranger on the subway. It almost feels as though she is actively avoiding making eye contact or conversation with me.

There is a nagging feeling of nausea in the pit of my stomach, my instincts screaming at me that something is wrong.

Of course, something is wrong, Ava. You are being held hostage – again.

Until I can figure things out, I just need to keep my head down and do as I am told. Play along and let this woman think that I am on her side of things. Bide my time until Renzo comes for me.

I know that he is going to come for me. I belong to him, and he will never let anyone else have me.

My eyes fixate on the city passing by the window. While I do not know where we are, it is apparent that we are no longer in the same area of the city. With every minute that passes, the buildings that we are driving by become increasingly dilapidated.

Chapter Thirty-Eight

LORENZO

As though he is more than aware this will be his only opportunity to share what he knows, Razmik begins to tell us everything as though we are the priest providing his last rites and he is receiving his final confession.

"I've been with the family a long time. Thirty years ago, I worked mostly as a driver. I was the one who drove Levon and his twins home from the hospital."

"Over the years, I probably spent more time with Karine and Karyan than he did. I drove them nearly everywhere I went to their concerts and sports and helped them with their homework. I'm not saying that I was a replacement for their father, but I loved those girls as though they were my own and they both knew it."

The words continue to spew from him between airy grunts as though he needs to relieve himself of this information more than we want it.

"When she was seventeen, Karine started sneaking around with that Tanaka kid. She promised me that she had ended things when I found out. Only, a few months later she came to me and begged me to get her out of this life. It wasn't until I learned that she was pregnant that I finally agreed."

"We both knew what a Gregorian carrying a Tanaka would mean. Back then no one would dream of these two families speaking to each other, let alone being civil for the sake of a child. Both of their lives were in danger, from both families. From all the families. So, I did what anyone would do, I helped her run. I got her a new identity and helped her disappear to save both of their lives."

His eyes dart around the room for approval of his good deed, approval that is not coming.

"I discreetly kept an eye on them and made sure they always had enough. When Karine disappeared, I struggled with myself for a long time about saving Avalie. She was in a shitty situation, but Karine had fully protected her from any knowledge of her previous life."

Sal's head drops and he shakes his head.

"I know it was shitty that I left her with that asshole. You don't need to tell me that. But she was safer with his drunk ass than she would have been if anyone had found out who she was. She is walking leverage against the families of both her parents. What family wouldn't want control of her?"

"For twenty-three years, I thought that I was the only person who knew this secret. A couple of months ago, Karyan somehow found out about what had happened with Karine. And then she found out about Avalie," he drops his gaze to the floor and takes in a staggered breath, "I've failed Karine, and I have been waiting for Karyan and Yuri to come for me since."

His gaze comes back up and meets mine, his eyes duller than before, "Then that asshole sold her to you and everything about this situation escalated. Karyan had to get her from you before Avalie had the opportunity to tell you who she really was, giving your family all the power."

"But you said Avalie doesn't know anything," Carlo's voice is questioning.

"She doesn't," Razmik replies, "but Karyan didn't know that. She started this war to create a distraction, allowing her time to put her plans into place and get her hands on Avalie."

"The fires?" Sal questions.

"All Karyan," Razmik answers, "She has been running all sorts of things lately. She has been fucking with everyone – fires, drug raids, basically anything she can do to be disruptive. It was never about the business. She has been doing it to create chaos and increase the strained relations between all the families."

Razmik continues, his body exhausted from losing the weight of this burden and the blood slowly pumping from his body, "I never actually thought that Yuri would put his daughter, a woman, in charge of his empire. But lately she has her hands in all different aspects of his business."

My eyes fixate on his and the life slowly fading from them, "Tell me where to find Ava and I will end this for you. Quickly."

"There is a family meeting at an old, abandoned church in Rockland County in about twenty minutes ago," Razmik struggles to push out the words, "It will be over before you could ever get there. Karyan will want to keep Avalie to herself. The most protected place she has is her penthouse suite at The Empire."

His pained eyes look at me, waiting for me to provide him with the mercy that I had offered. While it is not normally in nature, I uphold my promise. Pulling my gun, quickly place it against the bridge of his nose and pull the trigger.

Chapter Thirty-Nine

AVALIE

We drive for so long that I do not know if we are even still in the city. The SUV comes to a stop as we pull up in front an old church. If it were not for the sheer number of expensive cars parked in front of it, I would have assumed that it had been abandoned many years ago. Most of the windows are broken and the front doors are nearly hanging off the hinges.

Two large gentlemen open each of our car doors within seconds.

"Out," Karyan commands at me.

Following her demand, I slide from the backseat being careful to maintain my balance as my heels hit the gravel parking lot. Fully concentrating on staying upright on the uneven ground, I slowly join a very impatient Karyan on her side of the car.

With one in front of us and one behind, the large gentlemen escort us into the church. It is as rundown inside as it appears to be from the outside. The musty smell from lack of use mixed with urine is so strong that it turns my stomach. Cobwebs and dust cover nearly every surface, and several of the pews have been overturned.

There are a few men in suits sitting in some of the upright pews towards the front of the church. All heads turn as they hear the clicking of our heels on the wooden floors, and I feel as though they are all completely fixated on me.

"What is the meaning of this?" a man calls to Karyan from the alter as he stands. His stature and presence remind me a great deal of Sal. He is tall, both his hair and well-trimmed beard salt and pepper in color. And he is impeccably well dressed, in a suit that probably costs as much money as I would make in a couple of months.

Ignoring his question, Karyan continues to walk towards the alter at the front of the church. Although it has become obvious that I am not welcome here, I continue to walk behind her while trying to maintain her quick pace.

"Father," Karyan's voice dry as she speaks.

"Karyan," he nods at her before gesture lavishly at me, "I ask again, what is the meaning of this?"

"The meaning of what?" her voice still dry as she attempts to be coy.

"You are well aware that this is a meeting for family. Bringing outsiders is not accepted," he begins to reach for what I can only assume is a gun inside of his suit jacket.

"She is family," Karyan retorts to him, resulting in an immediate look of confusion on his face. His hand retreats from his jacket with a gun. Relief washes over me when he holds it to his side instead of pointing it at me.

"The fuck she is," he spits back, "I've never seen this bitch in my life. She is not a part of this family."

"That's where you are wrong father," her voice dry and cold again, "she is family. In fact, she is the future of this family."

"What the fuck are you talking about?"

"This is Avalie Gregorian."

I want to correct her and tell her that my last name is Taylor, but based on the tension in this room, I feel as though it is in my best interest just to keep quiet right now.

"She is Karine's daughter," Karyan continues, "and she is the fucking future of this family."

"What makes you think this bitch is so important?" Yuri quips back.

"She's Tanaka's daughter. He wants her, and he will do whatever the fuck I say to make that happen."

"That is ridiculous. Your sister would never..."

"Oh Daddy," her voice changes as she reaches into her purse, "Why do you think she left? And how old do you think this one is? I am going to need you to get on board with this plan of action very quickly."

"Karyan, this is crazy. Tanaka will never do what you say to get his bastard child back."

Without hesitation, she pulls the gun from her purse and fires three times at Yuri's chest. Both of my hands quickly cover my mouth in an attempt to catch the gasp that flies from it. I can feel tears welling in the corners of my eyes and my body is beginning to tremble as she places the gun back into her purse.

Turning to the men sitting in front of her, some in obvious shock, she addresses them, "Boys. In case you haven't figured it out yet, I am in charge now. This is my family. You can follow me or prepare to spend the rest of eternity rotting on the pews in which you sit."

As she finishes speaking the large men who escorted us into the church, pull their guns and point them towards the crowd.

"What will it be, boys?"

Chapter Forty

LORENZO

Walking from the poker room back to the car, the three of us determine that our best course of action is to head to Carlo's office. From there, we can learn everything we need to know about Karyan's penthouse.

I will be getting Avalie back, and soon.

Carlo calls a few of his guys and they start while we drive. They are as efficient as hell, because by the time we arrive about an hour later, they have printed out blueprints of the building and hacked into the security system.

Circling the table, I am impressed with their work. They have already begun cross referencing the security footage with the blueprints. There is a great deal of footage and numerous floors to map out, but several hours later we have finished. By the time we are done we know how many men are covering this building and where they are positioned.

Feeling my phone buzz, I pull it from my pocket.

DMITRYI

Yuri is dead.

Karyan has assumed control.

Instead of texting him back, I give him a call, "When did this happen?"

"Just now," he responds, "Maybe thirty minutes ago. Karyan took him out."

"Her own father?"

The phone is silent for a moment before Dmitryi finally replies, "Yes. She took him out to take control."

"What the fuck...?" I reply before ending our call.

While things are run differently between all of the families, there is one thing that I know to hold true for all of them – family above everything. You never go against your blood. You never betray your family.

The fact that she not only betrayed her blood, but managed to assume control without the rest of the family coming for her speaks volumes about how important Avalie is to all of the families.

I am dropping my phone onto the table when Sal glances over at me, "What's going on Lorenzo?"

"That was Dmitriy," I pause, taking a moment to still shake my head in disbelief, "Karyan killed Yuri, to take control of the family."

Even Sal doesn't have words to respond to my news, he simply stares back at me in disbelief. It is an unspoken rule that you never betray your family, and the punishment for betrayal is death. Yet somehow, she committed the ultimate family sin and is still alive.

Ideally, we would take several days, if not weeks, to plan a hit on another family like this, but I am not willing to risk Avalie being in this situation for that long. Right now, Avalie is leverage for Karyan. We need to get to her before she is no longer needed. Too much is unknown. If this shit wasn't already bad enough, it is only going to get worse with that crazy bitch in charge.

Chapter Forty-One

AVALIE

I do not know who is trembling more, me or the men sitting in the pews with guns pointed at their faces. She literally just killed her own father. I supposed he actually meant something to her, while I am a no one.

Why should I even remotely think that she will keep me alive?

Right now, I am a bargaining chip. She is going to use me to get what she wants out of the Yakuza. Once I am no longer of use for her, she will no longer have a need to keep me.

The one stop we made after the church solidified that for me. Karyan left me in the car with a few of her hired men. After she had been gone for twenty minutes or so, one of their phones rang and I could barely hear her through the other end, "Roll down her window, so he can see."

One of the men promptly rolled down my window. The fucking asshole sitting next to me shoved me against the door while grabbing my hair and using it to twist my face towards the building. After holding me there for a moment, he let go and the window promptly rolled shut. A few minutes later, Karyan returned to the car.

"For a man who has no proof that you truly are his," she scoffs, "It appears that Tanaka would move heaven and Earth to ensure your safety."

Since then, I have sat in silence the rest of the drive, while she discusses him allowing her free access to the port, and something about safe passage for all her shipments, with the armed assholes in the car with us.

I have no idea where we are until we drive through Times Square. While I am not personally familiar with the area, I at least know that we are back in Manhattan.

Does that do me any good? Probably not.

After driving a few more blocks, we roll up to a gated parking garage. The driver presses a button on his visor, and it slowly rolls open just long enough to let us drive through it. Once we park, my door opens and the asshole sitting next to me shoves me out of the car and into the arms of another armed asshole. He firmly grabs my arm and begins pulling me towards the elevator.

"Jesus Christ," I yell, "You don't have to fucking manhandle me, asshole. I'll fucking walk."

His grip tightens and he pulls on me so that I am looking up at his evil smile, "You're a mouthy little bitch, aren't you?"

I attempt to yank my arm back from him to keep walking, but his grip is too tight.

"Enough Ari," Karyan yells to him.

While he doesn't let go of me, his grip loosens a little and he stops dragging me behind him, allowing me to walk with him towards the elevator. When the doors open, Karyan and I enter with three of the armed men. The rest stay behind, but I do not know if it is because we will not all fit or they are headed elsewhere in the building.

When the elevator doors finally open, we immediately step into a large, luxurious apartment. I don't see much of it as I am pulled through the living room towards the opposite end of the building. The asshole pulling me opens the door and shoves me into the room.

"Fucking asshole," I yell back at him. I know I should be quiet and keep my head down, but I can't. I spent my life not bowing down to this shit, and I am not about to start now.

My words light a fire in him because it only takes him a second to cross the distance between us. His hand violently wraps around my throat, as he slams me against the wall, before crushing me with his body. His free hand slides down my body and along my hip.

"You might want to watch your mouth when Karyan isn't around to protect you," his words vile as he grinds his cock against me, "Or I can fill it to shut you up."

"Based on that limp noodle you're rubbing against me; I don't think you're capable of shutting up shit."

I have only a second to register that my words pushed him to far before his fist crashes into my face, everything immediately going black.

Chapter Forty-Two

LORENZO

Sitting around and waiting for nightfall for the past few hours has nearly killed me.

How it happened may not be conventional, but somehow Avalie has become my fucking world. I may have taken her life as a payment for a debt, but in reality that woman owns me. She owns my heart, and the mere thought of not getting her back safely makes my heart begin to race with panic. The concept of never touching her again fills me with an indescribable emptiness and rage.

This world is not prepared for me if I lose her.

It is just after midnight when our SUV's pull into Midtown, just down the block from where Karyan's penthouse is located. About two hours ago, one of

Carlo's guys watched through the security feed as they all returned here. Karyan and several armed men brought Ava up through the elevator. Once in the penthouse, they took her to a room upstairs in the back and two guards were posted outside of her door.

He assured me that she was okay, but I didn't believe him until a screenshot of her finally dinged through my texts. She is okay, or at least she appears to be unharmed. The look on her face is brave, but I know her — that face and those eyes. She is trying to be brave while hiding the fact that she is absolutely terrified. Ava is a smart girl, and there is no doubt that she is aware of the severity of the situation that she is in.

I hope you know I am coming for you, piccola pesca.

There are twelve of us as we climb out of the SUVs, and we leave three men behind with the cars for quick getaway. We were all dressed in black and armed to the teeth — pistols, semi-automatic rifles, small explosives. We are walking into this building fully prepared for war, ready to kill every last man to get back what is mine.

We split into two teams of six, half heading towards the front and my half heading towards the back. Luca's team is going to take the front, while mine will take the back. The plan is to breech both entrances simultaneously, and to make quick and quiet work of getting up to the penthouse. After scaling the chain-link fence, I pick the lock to the service entrance at the back of building.

The plan is to keep this as quiet as possible for as long as we can. I pull the door slightly ajar while taking a firm grip on the handle of my knife. Glancing down at my watch, ten seconds to go.

Nine...eight...seven...six...five...four...three... two...

A loud boom comes from a transformer just down the street, and the lights immediately go out for the majority of the block. Pulling the door open, I step inside and can immediately hear the chaos coming from Karyan's security detail.

"It's the whole block," I hear a calm voice through the radio of a guard standing just around the corner from me.

I pause, giving him the opportunity to respond to the man on the other end. As soon as he finishes, I step around the corner and plunge my knife between his ribs and into his lung while wrapping my hand over his mouth. Using the hand stifling his bloody cries for help as leverage, I pull the knife from his chest and immediately slide it across his neck before dropping him to the floor.

The service entrance to this building was poorly secured and guarded. It is either the oversight of a shitty security detail or a trap – both of which we are entering this building prepared for. Barring the potential for surprise, we have twenty-two flights of stairs to climb to reach the penthouse.

With my knife still firmly gripped in my right palm, I grab the rifle slung around my neck with my left hand to hold it against my body and begin taking the stairs two at a time. The five guys behind me all do virtually the same, as we make quick work of heading upstairs.

The only sounds in this stairwell are our boots stomping along the stairs and our heavy exerted breaths. It isn't until we reach the eighteenth floor that I realize just how eerily quiet it is. While it was going to be hit or miss for guards back here, I fully expected Luca's guys taking the front of the building to be met with some resistance. While my guys are good at their jobs, they aren't that good.

Bang. Bang. Bang.

As faint gunshots echo through the building, I realize my thoughts came too soon.

This changes things…

"Pick up the pace," I call back to the exhausted guys behind me. Gun shots mean they know we are here. They know what we are coming for, and that means that Avalie is now in danger.

The clang of metal reverberates through the stairwell as a fire door slams shut a few floors below us. It is immediately followed by the sounds of multiple sets of feet racing up the stairs to find us.

"Go," Marco yells over the loud stomping of their feet, "Get her, I will hold them off."

We all know that this might be a suicide mission for him, but *this* is what you do for the family. He turns and begins quietly moving down the flight of stairs while the rest of us try to reach for the fire door to the penthouse.

Gently pulling at the handle to the door, I am quite surprised to find it unlocked. That feeling does not change when I pull it open only to find a pistol shoved into my face.

They knew we were coming this way.

He must have anticipated that I would be alone, because his face is nothing short of complete shock as I move to the right just enough for Carlo to squeeze off three deafening rounds between me and the doorframe, dropping the man holding the gun to my face instantly.

More gunshots go off below us. The repeated pops echoing throughout the stairwell so loudly that the sound is disorienting. Through the noise, I can hear Marco yelling, but I am unable to comprehend any of what it is he is saying.

I feel a hand on my shoulder, which immediately refocuses me. I turn to see Carlo nudging me to proceed through the doorway and down the hallway. Grabbing the rifle slung around my neck with both hands, I step over the dead man laying at my feet.

Chapter Forty-Three

AVALIE

I am startled awake and for a moment I think it is just a nightmare of the other night, but I quickly realize that no one is coming to abduct me.

My face is throbbing and my head pounding as I push myself up from the floor.

What the fuck am I doing on the floor?

Fuck!

That asshole hit me.

Although based on our interaction, I guess, at least he only hit me.

My reflection in the mirror across the room catches me off-guard and I gasp at my face. The whole left side is crusted with dried blood from the cut on my cheek.

Behind the dried blood, is a massive bruise and swelling that is quickly forcing my eye shut.

Walking into the bathroom, I grab the towel off the rod and dampen it to clean the blood from my face. I cannot hold back the wince as I touch my own face, and tears well in my eyes as I delicately try to clean up the dried blood.

Even cleaned up, I look like I got the shit kicked out me.

Although, I guess I did just get the shit kicked out of me.

I pull open a few of the drawers, looking for something for this pounding headache.

Heading back into the bedroom, I begin to look for something to help me get out of here – anything. Pulling open drawers is futile, as they are all empty. I regret that I stopped carrying my pocket knife. While it might not be super useful, at least it was something.

Yeah, because it did you a lot of good with Renzo.

The city lights sparkle on the other side of the window and even though the light hurts my eyes, I am immediately drawn to them. I stagger across the room, my body moving as though I am drunk. Stumbling the last couple of steps, I catch myself as my palm presses against the cool glass.

Keeping my hand on the glass, I attempt to regain my balance. I walk along the wall of windows, pacing with my palm lingering on the glass as I try to figure out a way out of here. With how high up I am, the only way out is going to be through the door I came in.

As much as I want to cross the room to check to see if the door is locked, my body will not cooperate. I just want to lay down and sleep for a little while.

Fumbling my way back to the bed, my body nearly collapses into it. My eye lids are heavy as I slowly curl my body into a ball.

BANG BANG BANG!

Gunshots echo from a distance on the other side of the door.

Renzo...

...Is he coming for me?

Chapter Forty-Four

LORENZO

With Carlo at my back, we quickly make our way down the hall picking off any of Karyan's guys when we see them. By the time we make our way to the main area of the penthouse, we have left a trail of bodies in our wake.

We have eliminated every hired gun in this penthouse and been through every room except the one we watched them move Avalie into.

"Get Ava," Carlo yells over to me, "I'll do one more sweep to look for Karyan."

"Be careful," I call back to him before opening the door.

Stepping inside, I carefully sweep the room to ensure that the only other person in this room is Avalie laying on the bed. She doesn't move as I approach her, and I immediately think the worst.

Lowering my rifle, I pull my pistol from my waistband as I kneel on the floor beside her and gently brush her hair off her face. An angry growl grumbles from my chest as I take in her face. If I wasn't near certain that Carlo or I had already blown the face off whoever the guy was that did this to her, I would be on a hunting spree.

"*Piccola pesca,*" I whisper while gently stroking her face, "It's Lorenzo."

"Renzo," my name slurred as it passes over her lips.

Her eyelids flutter, but do not fully open.

"It's okay," I continue to stroke her hair.

"I knew you would come for me."

"What made you so sure?" I toy with her just to keep her talking. Both in part to her obvious concussion and that I have missed the sound of her voice.

"Because I'm yours," she replies, as I gently lift her from the bed and into my arms, "and you take care of what is yours."

I smile down at her as her arms wrap around my neck and she nuzzles her face into my chest. She is slightly incoherent, but she is absolutely correct. There is nothing I would not have done to have her body in my arms again.

"She okay?" Carlo questions as he steps into the room.

"She will be," I nod at him as I carry Avalie to the door, "Are you ready to get out of here?"

"Back the way we came?"

"That's our best option. Can you take the lead?"

"I got you brother."

Carlo calls over the radio to let the other guys know that we have Ava and are on our way out.

Raising his gun, Carlo takes the lead as we cross the penthouse towards the stairwell we climbed to get up here. Pushing open the door, Carlo steps through and holds it so that I can easily pass through with Ava.

We make it down four flights of stairs before we find Marco. His body is resting against the spindles of the railing with his chin slumped against his own blood-soaked chest.

"Fuck," Carlo bends down, "Marco?"

I watch as he slides his hand against Marco's neck to feel for a pulse. Before he is able to find one, Marco's head snaps up as he grabs Carlo by the throat. His grip only lasts for a moment before he realizes he has Carlo in his vice.

Grabbing Marco's hand, Carlo pulls his arm around his neck as he helps to lift him to his feet.

"Fuck," Marco groans.

"We're going to get you out of here," Carlo replies, "but I'm going to need you to help me get you down these stairs."

"Fuck you," Marco spits back, pulling from Carlo's grip, "I can do it by myself."

"The fuck you can, you stubborn bastard. You have at least three extra holes in you at the moment," Carlo yanks Marco's arm back over his shoulder.

It takes significantly longer to make our way down the stairs than we had anticipated, but we eventually make it to the ground floor. Carlo and Marco push through the door at the rear of the building first, and there is an SUV waiting for us.

Opening the rear door, I lay Avalie across the seat before opening the lift-gate. After helping Carlo get Marco into the back, I close the lift-gate and slide in next to Ava. Before I say a word, the SUV quickly accelerates away from Karyan's building.

"Jimmie, call the doc and have him meet us at the house," I turn my head towards the back of the SUV, "Carlo, keep pressure on his wounds."

I hold Ava against my chest, gently stroking her hair as we make it through the city streets and back to the estate in record time.

Chapter Forty-Five

LORENZO

Pulling into the estate, Doc is waiting at the garage as we pull the SUV into the garage. Several guys immediately help to pull Marco from the back and take him to the make-shift operating room we keep set up for Doc in the garage. Marco is barely dropped onto the table before Doc begins his work.

Quickly cutting Marco's clothes from his body, he determines that he has been shot four times. The two that hit his shoulder and flank went straight through – clean entrance and exit wounds. Doc is most concerned with the two that struck his bicep and chest, "We have to get these two out, and I'm going to need someone to assist me,"

"I'll do it," Carlo stands as he begins to roll up the sleeves to his shirt and pull on a pair of gloves.

Doc nods his head while injecting what I can only assume is some sort of anesthetic into Marco. I watch the two of them work diligently to remove the two bullets and stitch up his wounds with Ava sleeping on my lap. A couple of hours have passed by the time Doc is pulling off his bloody gloves.

"I don't want to make any promises," Doc's voice trembles, "but if he makes it through the night, he should pull through this."

Doc doesn't exactly work for us out of the goodness of his heart or because we pay him well. Originally, he got drawn into this life to pay back a very large debt owed to our family. At this point, he has seen and knows way too much to not be a liability, so he is forced to continue to work for us.

"We are good Doc," I gesture at him to come towards me, "I know you did you all could."

"What about his one?" He cautiously reaches towards Ava, not wanting to overstep.

"I am pretty sure it is just a concussion, but please take a look at her," I stand from the couch while laying Ava down so that Doc can examine her.

He is thorough in his examination and concurs with my assessment of the concussion. He places a couple of butterfly bandages on the gash running across her cheekbone.

"The cut doesn't need stitches, and should heal up just fine," he pauses, "That eye on the other hand is quite swollen. Definitely keep some ice on it for the next few hours. I wouldn't want this to permanently affect her vision."

Doc continues as I gently lift Ava from the couch, "She is going to need sleep, but make sure you wake her occasionally for the next twenty-four hours. After that, limited stress or activity for at least a few days. If she has any headaches or anything seems to be out of her norm, please call me immediately."

"Thank you, Doc," I extend my hand from under Ava's knees to shake his.

"I have to get back to the hospital," he breaks eye contact with me, "someone should stay out here with him. I'll be back in the morning to look in on him."

"Sounds good," I nod giving him the acknowledgement he needs to know that he is free to leave.

"I'll stay out here with Marco tonight," Carlo says from behind me.

Turning I see that he has already changed out of his blood-soaked clothes and into comfortable sweats. He walks around me and flops onto the couch I had been using for Ava.

"Go," he tips his head towards the door, "Get Ava inside and take care of her. I'll call you if anything changes with Marco."

"Call if you need anything, too."

Turning from Carlo, I carry Ava out of the garage and toward the house. The guard at the door opens it for me as I make my way up the stairs. After making my way upstairs, I open the door to my room.

I am pleased to see that the cleaners have taken care of everything in here – down to the pool of blood that was covering the majority of the closet floor. Had this room still been in disarray, I would have preferred to take Ava across the hall.

Delicately stripping her of her clothes, I let out a heavy sigh. A sigh of relief that the large mark on her face is the only physical harm she endured while she was away from me. Being mindful of her face, I help her sluggish body into one of my shirts.

"Renzo?" Her hand slides along my face and it feels as though every nerve in my jaw is connected to my heart.

"Shhhhh," I pull back the blanket and help her lay down before tucking her into the bed, "Rest now, *piccola pesca*, we can talk tomorrow."

Once she settles and begins to drift off, I run down to the kitchen. After filling a bag with some ice and grabbing a dish towel, I begin to head back upstairs to Ava.

"Lorenzo," I hear Sal's deep voice billow out to me, "we have some important things we need to discuss."

"Not now, Papa," the words pass over my lips before I realize the disrespect in them.

"Okay," his reaction, or lack of reaction, surprises me, "I am glad you were able to do the thing I couldn't, and you brought her home."

"Oh, Papa," my words fall short as he shuts the office door to hide the sullen look on his face.

Chapter Forty-Six

AVALIE

The click of the door wakes me from my sleep. Each beat of my heart echoes through my throbbing head and the slightest movement shoots pain through my face, yet an indescribable calmness washes over me as I struggle against the bright lights to realize that I am in Renzo's bed.

"You're supposed to be sleeping," Renzo's voice a soft, warm whisper.

"Then maybe you should be quieter."

The mattress shifts a little as Renzo sits on the edge of the bed beside me, "I'm glad to see the Gregorians didn't manage to tame the brat in you either."

A small chuckle escapes me, immediately followed by a groan from the pain it causes.

It is impossible to miss the look of worry lingering in his eyes. This monstrous, alpha-hole of man is scared – scared over me.

"Less talking," Renzo's voice sterner, as he gingerly presses the bag of ice against my face.

Wincing as I pull back, Renzo does not remove it from my face. Instead, he ensures that it stays flush against my swollen eye.

"You can take it," his voice sarcastically sultry as the corner of his mouth ticks upward.

Wrapping my hand over top of his, I help hold the ice to my face before replying, "Fucking asshole."

"Your fucking asshole," he climbs over me and lays on the bed. Still holding the ice to my face, he slowly pulls my body backwards until I am flush against him – my back to his front.

A small groan rises from my chest when I feel his warmth radiating through the blankets.

"Did I hurt you?"

"No, Renzo...," my words becoming sluggish as sleep slowly starts to take over again, "it just feels good to be here with you."

"I'm going to need you to get some rest, *piccola pesca*. Doctor's orders."

"Always...so...bossy!"

"Doc said no strenuous activity until your concussion heals," his arms tighten around me, "and I need you to get better."

"Because you're worried about me," my voice extremely coy.

"Yes," Renzo responds, "and because what I have planned to welcome you back home is definitely going to be strenuous."

His growing cock rubs against my ass.

"Now listen for once," he growls into my ear while pulling the ice from my face, "and get some fucking sleep."

"Fine," I shift getting comfortable both on my pillow and in his embrace, "but definitely don't get used to it."

The sun is barely shining through the curtains as I begin to wake up. While my head still feels heavy and my thoughts are slow, the constant thumping I went to sleep with has passed.

Slowly stretching, my arm feels behind me for Renzo, but he isn't there. Rolling over, I find myself alone in the bed. I open my mouth to call out for him...

"I'm right here, Ava," he steps from the bathroom. Beads of water drip from his wet hair, rolling down his chiseled body until they are absorbed by the towel slung low around his waist.

"I didn't want to wake you, but I need to go check on Carlo and Marco."

"Are they okay?" The words come out as fast as I scramble to sit up. A movement I quickly regret as the room begins to spin.

"Careful," Renzo reaches out to me, "Carlo is perfectly fine."

Relief washes over me, until I realize what he didn't say, "And Marco?"

"Doc pulled four bullets out of him last night," Renzo's words are cut short by my gasp, "but he made it through the night and Doc had said that would be the worst of it."

"I want to go see him," I slowly find my footing as I stand from the bed.

"No," Renzo walks towards me, "You need to get your sweet ass back in that bed."

"You can either help me go see him," I take a step towards the door, "or I can do it myself."

"For fuck's sake, woman," Renzo huffs, "Are you ever going to listen?"

"Probably not," my shoulders raise as I smirk.

"Will you at least put on some fucking pants?"

Chapter Forty-Seven

LORENZO

Ava's arm is wrapped in mine as we make our way from the house to the garage. Not nearly as deceptive as she thinks she is, I am well aware that she is using me as support to help her stay balanced.

Doc is just finishing up with Marco as we enter the garage.

"I know he pulled through the night, but how is he doing?"

Before Doc can answer, I can hear Marco arguing with Carlo about getting out the bed.

"He's a stubborn ass," Doc smiles, "but he is going to be perfectly fine. Try to keep him still so he doesn't pull at his stitches."

Walking past Doc and towards Marco, I yell out to him, "Would you just lay the fuck down?"

"Fuck that," he yells back pulling the various wires connecting him to medical equipment from his skin, "I've still got five fucking lives left, and I feel fine."

"Apparently no one is going to listen to me today," I grumble as Ava slides her arm from mine and walks towards Marco.

"Thank you," she leans towards him and places a gentle kiss on his cheek, "I know this happened because of me, and I will be forever grateful of the sacrifice you made to save me."

"What am I? Fucking chopped liver," Carlo calls over to Ava.

"I'm sorry, Carlo," Ava slowly walks towards him.

"Because I didn't get shot, I don't get a thank you," he smiles at her as she leans up to gingerly place a kiss on his cheek as well.

"Keep it in your pants playboy," I glare my eyes at him, "we've talked about this."

Carlo simply smiles a big toothy grin back at me.

"Since no one is going to rest in bed like they're supposed to, we might as well all head inside to get some breakfast."

"Fuck yeah, I could eat," Marco winces as he quickly stands from the bed.

Shaking my head, I slip Ava's arm into mine to begin the walk back to the house. I would question if Carlo was going to be able to handle Marco, but it appears that he will be walking on his own. Slowly, but on his own.

Sal and Luca are already in the kitchen getting a cup of coffee when the four of us enter the room.

"That's a stubborn fucking bunch you got there," Sal gestures at me.

"No shit, Papa."

Instead of the dining room, we all take seats at the smaller table in the kitchen. There is plenty of room for the six of us.

"I had some guys working on everything last night," Carlo speaks as he pulls coffee cups for the rest of us from the cabinet. Once pouring, he continues, "They have scoured the security footage from the penthouse and the entire building. There is no sign of Karyan, and they don't know how she got out.

"Hold up," Ava startles in her seat, "You mean you guys have no idea where she is?"

"It's okay," my hand grabs hers resting on the table, "you are safe here."

"You said that before," Ava scoffs back at me, "and you do remember how that turned out?"

"I'm not leaving your side. I will not make that mistake again. If she wants to come for you again, she is going to fucking come through me first."

"They are currently looking into CCTV footage from around the building to see if they can pick her out of the crowd," Carlo continues, "but so far, they haven't found anything.

Sal takes a sip of his coffee, "I've fielded several calls from elder members of the Armenians this morning. They are begging for forgiveness for her actions. What do you want to do, Lorenzo?"

His questions catches me off-guard. In all my years, he has never asked for my opinion without first letting me know his – so I knew what the correct answer was.

Sipping my coffee, I ponder for a moment before answering, "We give it to them."

All eyes at the table fixate on me as though I have suddenly lost it.

"We give it to them," I continue, "if they take care of the rest of their traitors and turn Karyan over to us."

Sal inquisitively arches an eyebrow at me and nods for me to continue, "We make it known they are turning her over to us. It lets the other families know we own them now and leaves her without any allies."

Standing from the table, Sal nods his head in approval, "I will go make the call. Lorenzo, join me?"

AVALIE

Renzo has been babying me and forcing me to keep it easy for the past week. Always the one to be in control, he has been adamant that we follow Doc's instructions and it's driving me crazy.

While he will not lay a finger on me sexually, he seems to have no problem doing so with his lips. More correctly, his words. He has talked so much filth to me this past week, I do not actually know if he has anything dirty left to say to me.

Pulling the plug from the drain, I step from the soapy water in the tub and towel myself dry. Wrapping the towel around my chest, I tuck the end securely as I look at my reflection in the mirror. While it is still slightly discolored, my eye is looking more like normal every day.

Pulling at the elastic holding in my messy bun, my hair cascades down my back as I step from the bathroom. I scream as I turn into the bedroom.

"Fucking hell," I shout at Renzo.

He is sitting shirtless on the edge of the bed. My eyes pan over his chest, once again taking in the details of the intricate art drawn over the hard ridges of his body. Following the lines of both his artwork and the ripples of his body, my eyes make my way to his lap.

"What is that?" my hand gestures to his lap.

"Doc cleared you today," his words slow, "but recommended I go easy on you at first."

Fuck...

The sheer thought of him having his way with me makes me wet.

"Towel," he demands in a deep, gravelly voice. A voice that has me dropping my towel to the floor within seconds, leaving me naked before him.

His eyes slowly graze over my body as a low grumble rises from his chest.

"Come. Get on the bed."

Doing as I am told, I cross the room towards him and sit on the edge of the bed. Renzo kneels in front of me as he pushes my knees apart. His hands kneed at my thighs as he places wet, teasing kisses up and down my inner thighs. I spread my legs further and tilt my hips, giving him more access to me. My breathing becomes restless as he continues teasing the flesh at the uppermost part of my thigh.

"I've missed the sweet scent of your arousal," Renzo bites at the sensitive skin on my inner thigh as he works his way closer my aching clit, "but what I've really missed is how sweet your fucking cunt tastes."

Before I have a moment to react to his words, his hands have pulled apart my lips and his tongue has begun a violent assault on clit. My hips writhe, riding his tongue as he devours me. Laying back on the bed, I continue to work my clit against the aggressive swipes of his tongue. His fingers firmly grip my thighs, holding me open for him, as he begins to suck on my clit. The sheer pressure has me on the verge of coming, but when his tongue begins to work in tandem, circling my clit while he sucks, I cannot hold back the orgasm that wracks through my body. My thighs shake, struggling to break free of his hold as he continues to painfully pleasure me through my orgasm.

My arousal is coating the scruff on his chin when he finally pulls his mouth from me.

"How are you feeling, *piccola pesca?*"

My breathing is so rapid, I cannot answer.

"Based on the look on your face, you're okay to continue?"

As I nod my head at him, he bends back down and disappears beyond the edge of the bed. I feel his hand slide down my left leg before he lifts it and places a gentle kiss on the ball of my foot. I feel him wrap something around my ankle before his hands are on my right leg. After another kiss to the bottom of my foot, I feel him bind something around this ankle too.

Renzo slowly stands, pulling on whatever is wrapped my feet lifting them into the air in front of him. A shiny metal bar is suspended between my spread legs by the leather cuffs he strapped around my ankles. Dangling from the center of the bar are two more leather cuffs.

Renzo presses the bar forward with one hand, while using his other to grab my left wrist. Pulling it up to the bar, he buckles the cuff. He repeats the process with my right arm. After pulling my body towards him, he slowly steps back to admire his work.

I am on my back, with my ass at the very edge of the bed. My legs are in a wide V, with my feet pointing up to the ceiling. The bindings around my wrists forcing me to hold my legs up for him.

"So fucking perfect," his voice low and raspy as he unbuttons his jeans, "all your holes on display and mine for the fucking taking. And I do intend to take them all."

Fuck.

"Lucky for you," he smirks, "Doc told me to be gentle."

Freeing himself of his pants, his cock is massive and ready. Grabbing the bar between my ankles, he pulls it towards him slowly forcing my body into a seated position. Holding my shoulder for support, he guides my feet to the side of the bed. His hands on my shoulders the only thing keeping me from tumbling forward towards the floor.

Renzo takes a step toward me, and the head of his cock is resting just below my face. He slowly lowers my shoulders, until his tip brushes against my lips. I part my lips and he lowers me, forcing me to take every inch of him into my mouth before he slowly lifts me off him. He repeats the leisurely motion over and over, tipping me forward until I swallow all of his cock, leaving him dripping with my saliva as he gently fucks my mouth.

"You look so fucking beautiful swallowing my cock."

A groan rises from his chest as he lifts me off of him and pushes my shoulders all the way back to the bed. My feet pointing towards the ceiling again, he grabs my hips and pulls me to him until his cock presses against my entrance. He pauses for a moment, before slowly sliding his saliva covered cock inside of me inch by inch.

Renzo's hands slide up and down my legs as he rocks his cock in and out of me. Applying a little pressure to the bar, his leverage slightly lifts my hips off the bed. The head of his cock now blissfully sliding along that spot inside that leaves me undone.

As the orgasm begins to build at my center, he opens his mouth. His saliva trickles from his gaping mouth all over my clit. His fingers use the moisture to glide over my clit, and my body begins to tremble as the orgasm shoots through me.

The orgasm does not stop him, Renzo keeps relentlessly rubbing over my clit until my legs are violently shaking – fighting against the restraint of the bar keeping me open to him.

"One more," his voice deep and firm, "be a good girl and give me another one."

His fingers glide around my clit as he continues to gingerly fuck me. The need for him to make me come again is nearly painful.

"I said give me another one," he rolls my clit between his fingers, "don't make me ask you again."

His fingers tighten their grip, pinching my already overly sensitive nerves sending me over the edge again, "Fuck…"

Renzo still does not stop. His fingers delicately continue to dance around my clit, leaving my body both yearning for more and trying to retreat from his touch. Gripping the bar that I am restrained to, every muscle in my body flexes as another orgasm fires painfully through each nerve in my body.

I am completely exhausted, my extremities burning, as I feel a cool liquid drip down the crack of my ass. I watch hesitantly as Renzo squeezes a generous amount of lubricant onto his fingers before he rubs them together.

Using a motion similar to the one he used on my clit, Renzo rubs his fingers around my tight hole before slowly pressing one of them inside.

My body reacts to the movements of his finger, light mewls mixing with my heavy breathing, prompting him to continue. Renzo adds a second finger, carefully stretching my hole to make it more accessible for his cock.

"You like my fingers in your tight little ass," his words turning from a deep gravelly whisper to a growl, "but you're going to love my fucking cock."

His fingers pull from me, leaving me suddenly feeling empty. My body tenses when I feel him press the head of his cock against me.

"Relax, *piccola pesca*," his words now soft, "Breathe. That's it. You're doing so fucking good. Let me in."

Renzo lets out of groan as I feel him push the head of his cock inside of me, stretching me in a way I didn't believe would be possible. With tender movements, he slowly works his cock in and out of my ass, allowing my body to get used to him.

Holding my hips steady, he begins to gently thrust in and out of my tight hole.

"Your tight little ass takes my cock so well, like it was fucking made for me," his words raspy between his increasingly heavy breaths.

His words and this foreign sensation have me quickly approaching another orgasm. My hips rock towards him, trying to increase the tempo and depth of his thrusts.

"More...Renzo," I plead breathily, "Faster."

Renzo quickly unbuckles the restraints binding my wrists to the bar.

"You don't want faster," he flips me onto my stomach, tucking my knees beneath me as he slides the length of himself back into me, "You want it deeper."

"Fuck!" I cry out from the increased sensation of this position.

Renzo's fingers dig painfully into my hips. His grip ready to relentlessly slam his cock into me, yet he continues to be tender with his thrusts.

My breathing intensifies as my hips rock needily to meet his thrusts. His hand reaches between my thighs and begins rubbing my clit, immediately sending me over the edge, causing my arms to collapse beneath me.

Holding me tightly, Renzo's hips quiver against me as he empties himself inside of me, filling me with his cum.

Still fully seated inside of me, I feel Renzo tugging at the straps around my ankles. As he releases the second buckle, the bar falling to the hardwood floor with a clang. Renzo slowly pulls himself from inside of me, causing his cum to trickle down my thigh.

"I will never get tired of watching my cum drip from you," he whispers against my neck, before climbing onto the bed and dragging my limp, exhausted body into his embrace.

Renzo's lips pepper soft, wet kisses along the nape of my neck as he holds me against him.

"You are mine," he whispers against my ear.

"Yours," I exhale as I drift off to sleep.

Chapter Forty-Nine

LORENZO

This city has been flipped upside down since we took the penthouse last week. They dynamics between the families has shifted dramatically.

Sal negotiated a truce with the remaining members of the Armenians. Not being the type to allow disobedience, they took it upon themselves to rid themselves of anyone who turned on Levon. While what is left of their family is significantly smaller than a few days ago, what they do have left is tight and loyal.

They have also been working in tandem with Carlo and Marco to track down Karyan. Carlo and Marco have been with each other nearly day and night since the penthouse, searching diligently for any hint of her. Leads have brought them close a few times, but she keeps managing to stay a few steps ahead of us. We are nearly certain that she still has someone on the inside feeding her details and keeping her advised of our moves.

Neither the Botticellis nor the remaining Gregorians have any intention of ending the search. She will always be a threat for Ava, and because of that I will not rest until I put her to death with my own two hands.

The Yakuza, mainly Tanaka, have been reaching out relentlessly. The conversations are under the guise of a truce over hitting our estate or working together, but the reality is that he is trying to get to Ava. She has been clear that while he may be her blood, he is not her family. Her blood family died a long time ago, and we are her family now.

Things with the Yakuza are staying civil, at least for now. We are keeping a close eye on them. If they were bold enough to strike us at home once, we would never assume they would not make a move like that for her again.

Dmitriy has been significantly quieter in comparison, but due to his father's declining health he has also quickly been stepping into the role as the head of his family. As someone who has slowly been learning those ropes for years, I know that his hands are currently quite full.

Things between us are good, actually more civil than they have been in years. He has not so subtly hinted a few times that he needs to speak with me about the future of our families and how we can work together.

Sal and I have been sitting on the couch, sipping bourbon, and discussing the recent changes happening around the city for the past few hours in his office. The sun set hours ago and the moonlight is now peeking through the curtains.

"Your sister and Dante should be arriving in a couple of hours," Sal takes a large gulp of his drink, "I'm going to wait up for them."

The area they were hiding out in was desolate, and it took days for us to manage to reach them after things settled down, and I know that he is quite anxious for his princess to return home.

"You on the other hand should go to bed," he reaches for my glass.

"I'm not drunk," I pull the glass away, "and I'm not a child with a bedtime."

Snatching the glass from me, he retorts, "Maybe not, but you are fucking stupid."

My mouth gapes slightly at his insult.

Standing from the couch, he sets both of our glasses on the table.

"You have a beautiful woman lying in your bed right now, and you're sitting her drinking with an old man," he cracks a smile, "Now go to bed. I'll wait up for your sister."

I have never been one to disobey the Capo Dei Capi, and I figure now is not the time to start.

"Just fucking do it already," he calls to me as I step into the hallway.

After a brief detour to the bag of tools I keep ready in the garage, I head upstairs.

Opening the door, I am greeted by the sight of Ava on the bed. She is on top of the sheets, her body resting against the headboard as she reads. She is so engrossed in the book she is currently reading that I am not certain if she even realizes that I entered the room.

Walking toward the bed, my eyes flow over her body, starting at her delicate powder pink toenails and continuing up her long, lean legs. While they are different than the normal stringy thongs I tend to find her in, I quite like the white lacy boy shorts that are barely covering her ass. A snug white tank top attempts to cover her, but her pert, pink nipples are visible through the thin fabric.

Stepping beside her, my fingers wrap around her throat, immediately drawing her attention away from the pages in front of her. Gripping her tightly, I lean down until my lips are dusting over hers as she pushes against my grip to take in my kiss.

Chapter Fifty

AVALIE

I was so enthralled with the novel in front of me, I didn't realize Renzo had entered the room until his fingers wrapped around my neck. My breasts heave as his lips brush over mine like the dusting of a feather, barely making contact, as his grip keeps me from closing the distance between us.

He finally closes the small distance between us, and my lips part allowing him the access to my mouth we both want him to have. Our tongues and lips collide, as we kiss each other with a violent need — as though the air we are sharing is how we manage to keep breathing. Renzo pulls away with my lower lip firmly held between his teeth, biting down hard before letting go.

A small yelp comes from my mouth as he breaks the skin. Pulling my lower lip into my mouth, the metallic taste of blood coats my tongue. Licking over the bite, my eyes meet his.

"Do you like the pain?" His thumb slides over my bloody lower lip as his eyes fill with lust.

"Yes," I answer quietly, feeling my heart begin to race.

"Does my pain bring you pleasure, *piccola pesca?*"

"Yes," my body aching for him as I watch him lick my blood from his thumb.

His hand slides under my jaw as his fingers take hold of my chin, "Do you want me to pleasure you?"

Barely able to push out a response through my rapid breathing, I muster, "Yes."

Using my chin to guide me, Renzo leads me from the mattress to the bedpost. Leading me backwards, until my back is flush against the post he bends forward. Expecting him to kiss me again, I part my lips, but his travel toward my ear.

"Arms up," the two deep and demanding words shoot excitement straight to my core and I stretch my arms above my head. The cuffs hanging above me wrap around my wrists. Goosebumps erupting down my back with each click, as Renzo slowly tightens them.

Standing on my toes, my pussy clenches as I watch Renzo roll up the sleeves to his shirt exposing his forearms. My breath hitching with anticipation as he browses the various items in the armoire.

Renzo turns and begins walking toward me, striking the black leather slapper against his palm with each step. The crack echoes around the room over his heavy footsteps.

"I expect you to count my marks," he slowly turns my body dragging the slapper softly over my skin, "In return, I will make you come for every mark I leave on your body."

The leather cracks across my ass and I let out a loud yelp.

"Count," Renzo demands as he strikes me again.

"T...Two," I cry out.

"Good girl," his hand rubs over the marks left on my cheek.

He steps back, and I take a deep breath just as the leather strap snaps against my upper thigh.

A raspy, "three," explodes from my mouth as I exhale my breath.

Two rapid strikes hit my unmarked cheek. My toes curl, thighs clench and my head drops back as I moan out an airy, "Four...five."

"So beautiful, all marked for me," Renzo drops the slapper on the bed and drops to his knees behind me, his lips and tongue immediately on the marks covering my ass and thigh.

He spins me and pulls my panties to the side. As his tongue licks across my cunt, his hands shred the lace, causing the fabric to fall to the floor. Grabbing my thighs, he throws them over his shoulders as he fervently devours my clit. My hands struggle to hold the chains binding me to the bedpost and my heels dig into his back as I come across his tongue.

"One," he smirks deviously, before firmly grabbing my ass and pulling me back to his mouth. He continues to bite and lick my clit, as though he is starving man and I am his last meal.

My thighs flex, tightening them around his face as I scream through my release. He continues to lap at me as my hips ride against his face, nearly unable to withstand his continued assault on my clit. Every muscle in my body begins to twitch and my hands lose their grip on the chains, as he makes me come against his mouth again.

Sliding me from his shoulders, Renzo removes his boxer briefs. As I struggle to maintain my footing, he grabs my thighs and wraps them around his waist as he slides his full length inside of me.

"Always so wet and tight," he growls into my ear as he lifts my ass. The movement both sliding me up his length and providing me the opportunity to grab ahold of my restraints, "Hold on."

Renzo lets go of my ass, and I am impaled on his cock causing us both to moan loudly. Slowly continuing to thrust into my dangling body, Renzo grabs his knife from the bed and uses it to remove my tank top.

The knife still in his hand, he grips my hips and uses them as leverage to violently thrust into me.

"Who owns this sweet fucking cunt?" he sputters between his rapid breathing and thrusts.

"You," I scream as I come again, "It's yours."

Slowing his thrusts until he is barely moving inside of me, he slides the cold metal of the knife between our bodies and along my breast.

"And who do you belong to?" His question possessive yet tender.

"You. I belong to you," I pant through my still heavy breaths.

Lifting the knife until the tip of the blade is dimpling my skin, about to pierce it, "Are you sure?"

"Always."

Wrapping his free hand around my waist for support, his hips slowly rock, sliding himself in and out of me as he presses the knife harder breaking the skin. He pauses for a moment, continuing the gentle thrusts of his cock, before proceeding with the blade. I watch and wince as he intricately carves his initials over my left breast, *LB*, marking me as his forever.

Blood trickles from the letters, down my chest, as he turns the knife towards himself, the tip piercing the skin of his left pec. He buries his cock inside of me and grits his teeth as he carves into his own flesh before dropping the knife to the ground. When he drops his hand, I can see the marks he left behind. *AB*.

"I don't mean to ruin this grand gesture," my eyes drop to his chest, "but those aren't my initials."

"No?" his lips brush along jaw, to my ear, and he whispers, "but they will be...Mrs. Botticelli."

His lips and teeth gingerly travel down my neck, his hands roaming my body, as he upholds his promise of making me come for every mark he left on me.

I hope you enjoyed Lorenzo and Avalie's story!

If you did, the best support you can give to an indie author, like myself, is to tell others about my book. Reviews left on Goodreads, Amazon, or anywhere else you are comfortable truly mean the world to me.

* * *

Next up in this series is the story of Venecia, Lorenzo's little sister, in *Capo Dei Capi's Daughter*.

Ignite The Fire (Burning Fire: Book One)

Scorched Earth (Burning Fire: Book Two)

COMING IN 2023

More of the Botticelli Brotherhood

Capo Dei Capi's Daughter

Indebted To The Enemy

Falling For The Mafia Dom

I hope you enjoyed Lorenzo and Avalie's story!

If you did, the best support you can give to an indie author, like myself, is to tell others about my book. Reviews left on Goodreads, Amazon, or anywhere else you are comfortable truly mean the world to me.

* * *

Next up in this series is the story of Venecia, Lorenzo's little sister, in *Capo Dei Capi's Daughter*.